# Drop Dead, Gorgeous!

# Drop Dead, Gorgeous!

## MaryJanice Davidson

KENSINGTON PUBLISHING CORP.
http://www.kensingtonbooks.com

BRAVA BOOKS are published by

Kensington Publishing Corp.
850 Third Avenue
New York, NY 10022

ISBN 0-7582-1204-6

First Kensington Trade Paperback Printing: May 2006
10 9 8 7 6 5 4 3 2 1

Printed in the United States of America

*This book is for Sam, but not Scott. It's also for Jenny, the first woman I ever met who had no idea how beautiful she was. And for her beautiful sister, Jessica, who knows why . . . oh, hell, we'll just throw the whole Lorentz family in there. Frankly, they're all a pretty good-looking bunch.*

# Acknowledgments

Thanks to my agent, Ethan Ellenberg, for helping to make this book happen. I just write 'em. He does the hard stuff. Really! Given a choice between writing a book and reading a contract, guess which one I'll pick every time.

I have read that having a bad agent is worse than no agent at all, but thankfully, I don't know from bad agents. I also have no idea, thanks to Ethan, about bad contracts.

I mean, not to go on a whole rant here, but have you seen the font used on some of those publishing contracts? I get a headache just thinking about it, but not only does he have a gift for contract-ese, he has a gift for keeping me out of trouble. His enthusiasm, accessibility, and kindness are priceless beyond rubies.

Thanks also to my husband, a tireless sounding board, and my friend Jessica (another beautiful woman who does not know her worth), who thinks nothing of keeping her cell phone on her nightstand in case I want to call at 4:00 A.M.

I am blessed.

Finally, special thanks to my editor, Kate Duffy, for also being my sounding board and sending me cyber-Kleenex this fall. I love this book, but it was a difficult one to write. Kate knew, and if she ever feared what I was going to produce, she never let on. God bless the inscrutable editor.

*"The wrong war, at the wrong place, at the wrong time, and with the wrong enemy."*

—Omar Bradley

*"You know what it takes to sit across the table from a man, listen to him talk, look into his eyes . . . and then blow his brains all over the wallpaper?*

*"Nothing.*

*"And the more of that you have, the easier it is."*

—Andrew Vachss,
*Dead and Gone*

*"Always forgive your enemies . . . nothing annoys them so much."*

—Oscar Wilde

# Author's Note

This is the second book set in the Gorgeous universe. If you're standing in the bookstore trying to decide whether to buy this or not, let me assure you that *Drop Dead, Gorgeous!* is a stand-alone book, and you certainly don't need to read the first one to figure out what's going on.

But you don't have to take my word for it. In fact, you shouldn't take my word for it. Who am I? Someone who gets paid to spin yarns for a living . . . better check to make sure your wallet is still in your purse. Instead of taking my word for it, you should pick up the first book in this series, *Hello, Gorgeous!*

Go ahead. Reach for the shelf. The D's. Davidson. I'm usually in the middle of the shelf. Janet Dailey's books are probably to the left, and Jude Deveraux is to the right.

Anyway, reach out, grab *Hello, Gorgeous!*, read it, then read this one. And then you'll know I was telling the truth: this book really does stand alone. Although it's nice to find out how things began, don't you think?

You haven't bought it yet? Well, that's all right. I can bring you up to speed in just a couple of paragraphs. And it's fine if you didn't want to buy it. Really! I don't mind. I'm making the mortgage payments on my hovel, and the kids' rickets have nearly cleared up. Don't give it another thought. We're all fine.

No go, huh? Well, good for you. Paperbacks are getting more expensive all the time. There's always the library. (That sound you heard was my editor's head blowing up.)

Anyway. This book takes place about two years after the

events in *Hello, Gorgeous!* In that fine, upstanding work of clarity and vision (I'm expecting a call any day from the Pulitzer people), we met Caitlyn and Dmitri. Caitlyn was a pretty ordinary gal—smarter than she liked to let on, opinionated, a small-business owner (the hair salon Magnifique), single, loath to work out.

Then there was an accident, and then there was the O.S.I., and then there was The Boss. Caitlyn woke up in a hospital bed fundamentally changed; she had been infected with nanobytes. (Nanobytes=the twenty-first century version of bionics.)

The good news: she would not be breathing through tubes for the rest of her life. The bad news: the government-funded think tank, the O.S.I., expected her to work for them. Save the world on occasion. Show up at staff meetings. Wear a tacky, government-issued I.D. card. Unending horror.

What with one thing or another, Caitlyn ended up going after the only other person on the planet who was nanobyte-enhanced: Dmitri Novatur, code named The Wolf. She did this a) to get The Boss off her back, and b) because O.S.I. personnel were turning up dead, which wreaked havoc on the staff meetings.

In between catching bad guys, falling in love, running Magnifique, and trying to stay out of The Boss's clutches, we met Jenny, her assistant, and Stacy, her best friend. These women kept Caitlyn grounded as only the best of friends can; a woman who will tell you your butt looks big in peach is priceless beyond compare.

Caitlyn (saddled with the annoying code name Mirage because, as The Boss explained, no one ever knew if she was going to show up for work or not) saved the world (multiple times), got the guy (multiple times), and lived through the horror of her best friend falling for The Boss.

And that's about where we left off.

P.S. Nanobyte technology in the "real world" appears to be beyond our grasp, at least as far as Dmitri and Caitlyn are concerned; but there are still disastrous wedding luncheons every day, all over the world.

# Prologue

*The Snakepit*
*1430 hours*

"It has to be done."

"Yes, ma'am."

"Done now. Right now."

"Yes, ma'am."

"This has been on my To-Do list for a while. You know that."

"Everyone knows that, ma'am."

"Right. So nobody's going to think I'm doing it—finally—just because he's getting married to That Woman, right?"

"Right, ma'am."

"Because She has nothing to do with it."

"Got it in one, ma'am."

"Okay, then. So. Do it."

"Ma'am. I'll see to it myself."

# Part One

# WITHIN*

*Defined by *Merriam-Webster* as: 1. in or into the interior; 2. inside.

# Chapter 1

*The Grand Hotel*
*Minneapolis, Minnesota*

Jenny Branch watched as her boss was gently restrained from committing homicide.

"I have to do it now," Caitlyn James cried. "If I don't do it now, they'll—ugh!—do it. Do you know what that *means*?"

"They'll be husband and wife, pet," Caitlyn's husband, Dmitri, replied, catching her small fist and kissing it.

"*Don't say that*. Like they haven't already been doing it. Because they have! I had to gouge out my retinas when I accidentally walked into the kitchen at the wrong moment." Caitlyn seemed unaware that her husband had picked her up by the elbows and held her effortlessly off the ground as her small feet swung and kicked. "But that was sex. Nightmarish, disgusting sex. But still. The sex I could tolerate."

"What a charming liar you are, my love."

"Well, I was almost getting used to it. A teensy bit used to it. But marriage? Him? Marrying my best friend? No chance in hell. If I was ever going to kill him, I've got to do it now. So put me down already."

Jenny sighed again, and they both looked. "Sorry," she

6 *MaryJanice Davidson*

covered. "I love weddings." In fact, she hated them. Just what every single woman needed: a reminder that she would die alone, until the cats found her.

She was reminded, again, of her favorite movie, *When Harry Met Sally*, and the lines she thought applied to her in particular: "Suppose nothing happens to you. Suppose you live out your whole life and nothing happens. You never meet anybody, you never become anything, and finally you die one of those New York deaths which nobody notices for two weeks until the smell drifts into the hallway."

Not that she was from New York; she was a small-town Minnesotan, born and bred.

*(Who's going to want you?)*

But the rest of it applied to her.

*(You're not smart enough for college—stick with modeling.)*

It's why she was a dog person.

She shoved her thoughts from unnpleasantries and focused on the wedding, and her friends. Not that Dmitri was really anyone's friend—not even Caitlyn's, she sometimes thought.

But it didn't seem to matter; Dmitri and Caitlyn were so perfect for each other. And they would have the most glorious children. And Caitlyn hadn't even been trying to get married! She had loved being single, especially after getting free of her parents like that. Jenny suspected that was why she had been drawn to the tall, sarcastic, sometimes-annoying owner of Mag, the super-salon in St. Paul. They both had something in common: rotten parents.

Then Dmitri practically falls into Caitlyn's lap at her new job—or maybe she fell into his, Jenn never got all the details—and boom! A big, expensive wedding. In Lithuania!

Followed, in an annoyingly short time, by Jessica's wedding to The Boss.

It just wasn't fucking fair, and she knew it was petty, but

it was in her own head, and she was allowed to be petty there if nowhere else, right?

"I'd love it if you tried to make me put you down." Dmitri was breathing that sexy European accent right into Caitlyn's ear, and she was liking it plenty, too, the whore, but at least she wasn't screeching anymore.

"You guys, I don't really think—" Jenny peeked through the curtain again. The use of a curtain, rather than a door, to separate the bridesmaids (to wit: Caitlyn) from the groom (to wit: The Boss) was making her nervous. "I don't think Dmitri's supposed to be back here."

"And *I* don't think this farce of a wedding is supposed to be taking place—there's only a million other nicer things to do in Minneapolis on a gorgeous day like today—but here we all are."

"It's pouring rain."

"So?"

"Caitlyn, do we have to go through this again?" Jenny tried to keep the exasperation out of her voice. Caitlyn was, for all her faults, still the boss.

"I guess I'm the only person who sees all the unique horribleness in the situation," Caitlyn hissed, which made Dmitri snort briefly with laughter.

A new voice interrupted the *faux* fight. "Jimmy, hon, you are totally replaceable. You know that, right?"

Dmitri put down the maid of honor. Jenny turned. The bride was standing on the opposite end of the sitting room, just closing the far door behind her. The room itself, a plush, brocaded thing with too many chairs, looked far more dressed than the bride.

"Stop calling me Jimmy," Caitlyn said, newly distracted.

The bride ignored her. "I'm surprised you two didn't hear me clomping up the stairs—you got ears like hounds."

"We were a little preoccupied," Dmitri said, trying not to

stare at the golden brown tops of Stacy's breasts, which were barely held in by the creamy bustier.

"Yeah, and now we're busy saving your life. Again! Though metaphorically this time."

"Actually, boss, more figuratively than metaphorically. A metaphor is defined as the substitution of an idea or an object with another idea or object. For example, 'the aggressive couple howled at the moon' would be a metaphor."

"Jenny, honey, I love you, but we got no time for your spooky smartness. I need help!" Stacy spoke gently enough, but her voice spiraled up into panic at the end. "The seamstress is late with my dress. My underwear is at least a size too small. And I just had to break up a fistfight between the caterer and one of the waiters."

"Nonsense," Dmitri, a man like all men in at least one thing, replied. "Your underwear is perfectly sized. Speaking on behalf of grooms everywhere, you don't need another stitch. Now go on out there and swear eternal love to the luckiest man on earth."

"That's going to cost you," Caitlyn muttered.

"Well spoken, my dear. Very well . . . . to the *second* luckiest man on earth. The important thing is, you're dressed."

His wife elbowed him in the ribs. "I see your point, Stace. But maybe you should look at this as more like an omen, you know?"

Stacy crossed the room with terrifying speed. Given that she had no enhancement, technological or otherwise (she didn't even like to run on the treadmill), it was an impressive move.

She jammed a finger under Caitlyn's chin (the nail, Jenny noted, was painted bright blue) and said in a low, terrifying voice, "We've been over this. I'm marrying him. Now you can stand up or you can get out of my way. *Don't* make me go through this with you again."

"Okay," Caitlyn said with uncharacteristic meekness, but then, who wanted to get a bright blue fingernail jammed into their eyeball? And on such a shitty day? "Sorry. Don't, uh, do anything rash."

"Don't talk to me about rash, girlfriend. You don't know from rash."

"This is true," Caitlyn admitted and, for a wonder, had no further comment.

"While we're waiting for the seamstress, maybe we could touch up your hair a little," Jenny suggested. Among other things. The bride *was* looking a little stressed; Jenn could see the sweat beading her temples.

"I have to get dressed first. Besides, hon, I've got work for all of you," she added, nodding to Dmitri. "You need to go down to the kitchens and make sure no more fights break out."

"Hmmph," Dmitri said, allowing himself one last lingering look at her cleavage.

The bride ignored him. "The boneheads haven't frosted my cake yet, God knows why—"

Caitlin raised her hand like a kid in school. After a pause, Stacy said, "Caitlyn?"

"I've mentioned that all these things going wrong are an omen, right?"

"Shut up. Why don't you go down with Dmitri?"

"Why don't I?"

"And Jenny, I need *you* to track down the decorator, or whatever the cake-toppie-thingie-person is called. You can play with my makeup and hair after that . . ." she added, pointing to a perfectly beautiful, slicked-back ponytail with rich brown curls swinging at the back, curls that had been twined with ribbon the exact color of her missing dress. There were benefits to having friends who worked in a salon.

"Don't touch your hair," Caitlyn ordered.

"I'm *not*. And the dress will have arrived by the time she gets back. *It will*. And then the show will go on. God willing, the show will go on."

Given their marching orders, they all got to work.

# Chapter 2

Jenny found the cake, but no cake decorator. "She had to leave," a doleful waitress informed her. "She was getting a migraine."

"She couldn't decorate the cake, *then* leave?"

The waitress, filling silver-rimmed plates with petits fours, didn't look up. "No way. She tried that once, but when she gets that way she sees double."

"But—the cake?"

The waitress, who had finished with the tiny cakes and was now stacking empty glasses on the counter between them, actually shivered. "Just the thought of it. Curds of meringue everywhere—even the ceiling! The cake looked like someone punched it, and then had sex with it."

"So . . . what? What's the plan? We can't serve it to the guests like this." Jenny eyed the cake, a four-tiered confection of what appeared to be vanilla sponge. It was neatly put together, and there were several bowls beside it, all full of perfectly whipped frosting.

"One of the waiters did a jelly roll for his nephew, once. We're trying to find him."

*Oh, great. Just the perfect touch. Maybe he'll stick a goddamned pony in the middle.* Jenny sighed, and pushed up her sleeves.

Pity. It was a great bridesmaid's dress, as nice as the one she'd worn for Caitlyn's big day. A cream-colored pattern with roses embroidered onto the fabric, puffed sleeves, and a scooped neckline that made her feel like a milkmaid but which everyone else informed her was charming. It looked dynamite on Caitlyn, too; but then again, what didn't?

*You've got to get hold of this unreasonable, continuous jealousy. You've got to.*

"Hey, what's the Russian guy doing wandering around back here?" the waitress whispered. "Is he, like, a former KGB agent?"

"He's Lithuanian," she replied, picking up a bowl of frosting and a spatula, testing it for thickness. *Mmmm . . . butter-cream . . .* "He's on some mission or another from the bride."

"I've got a mission for him."

"Yes, too bad he's married," Jenny said sweetly, accidentally forking a large clot of frosting onto the woman's spotless shoulder. "Oopsie."

Jenny stepped back from the cake, her back aching like someone had stuck a few spatulas in it, right between her kidneys. But the thing was done, anyway, even if she was covered in buttercream.

From the increase in hustle around her, she figured the witching hour was near. Or, at least, the time on the invitations: 2:00 P.M.

The door between the kitchen and one of the small dining rooms swung open.

"She's back here," Caitlyn said, and then they all burst into the kitchen and, at the sight of an obviously tense bride, the entire waitstaff managed to disappear at once, leaving the makings of an omelet bar. Jenny was left to explain the cake.

"Well," she began, scraping frosting off her elbow, "the

gal who decorates the cakes had to go home. And they didn't have a substitute. And there was a migraine involved. So I sort of took it upon myself."

At the blank stares, she elaborated. "To do it, I mean. They had everything put together and all the frosting made— I just had to color some of it. I found a whole rainbow of food coloring in the pantry."

In the continually creepy silence, Jenny rushed ahead. "And I just—just thought—because of the dresses—and all that talk about your grandma's garden and how you wished she could be here but she's not—obviously she's not, since she passed away last year—anyway, I thought you might like this."

"This" was the four-tiered cake, with snow-white frosting smoothed on, and lilacs and tulips piped onto the tiers from the bottom up, as if they were growing onto the cake. The lilacs were the faintest shade of lavender, the tulips were dark pink, and the leaves and stems were the shimmery green of a spring forest on the first really hot day.

She had destroyed her own bouquet (purple tulips, pink and yellow alstroemeria lilies) to create a small crown of real flowers for the top tier.

They stared at the cake.

They stared at her.

They stared some more.

*Nuts*, Jenny thought in despair. *Fucked up.* Why had she believed this would be a good idea?

Stacy started to cry, and moved to attack—no, hug—her, but Jenny held her at arm's length. "I'm head to toe frosting," she pointed out. "You'll ruin your dress."

"Like I care?" she said, crying and laughing at the same time. Since she couldn't hug Jenny, she jumped up and down. "Oh, Jenn, you genius! You saved my reception!"

"Well." She coughed modestly, feeling the blood rush up

to her eyebrows. She scanned the kitchen desperately for a corner to hide in. "It wasn't all that much . . ."

Caitlyn was circling the cake admiringly. "I didn't even know you could do this. Did you take a class?"

"No. My mother did this for a living."

Caitlyn shot her a quick glance, but Stacy bubbled on, and thankfully, the moment was lost. "It's wonderful! It's just what I wanted. Thank you, thank you so much." Ignoring Jenny's wrigglings to keep away, Stacy wrung her hand until it was sore. And then it dawned on her . . .

"Hey! You're dressed."

"And a damn fine-looking woman I am, too," Stacy replied, preening. She spun for Jenny's benefit, showing the deeply scooped back and the almost as deeply scooped front. Stacy liked any gown to display all cleavage.

"That's a very . . ." She eyed the enormous meringue skirt. "Big dress."

"Oughta be, for what my honey paid for it."

Jenny had been wondering about that. A ceremony and reception at the Grand, a four-figure dress. Not cheap. And Stacy was a college student, pre-law. Her folks raised horses; fulfilling, but not much money involved.

"If he's going to suck you so deeply into his personal life," Caitlyn muttered, "the least he can do is foot the bill for the wedding."

Jenny tried not to roll her eyes. "If you're dressed, then everything's ready."

Caitlyn was still prowling around the cake. "More than ready—God, that thing looks delicious."

"So . . ." Jenny paused, and when they didn't seem to catch on right away, added, "Why are you all out here? I think you scared the waitstaff away. Possibly permanently."

"To come get you, of course," Caitlyn said impatiently. "It's not a wedding if one of the bridesmaids is missing."

She eyed the tattered remains of Jenny's bouquet. "It's not that important, but, hmm, I don't suppose we have an extra bouquet lying around, do we?"

"I think the florist is still here," Stacy replied. "But I'd rather Jenny was empty-handed than have a naked cake."

"Don't say naked," Caitlyn commanded. "This day is going to be enough of a strain."

"Shut up, Jimmy."

"*You* shut up."

"You can't tell the bride to shut up on her wedding day."

"Sure I can. And enough of the 'it's my special day, I get my way in everything' crap. You're more like Bridezilla than a blushing flower."

"Ladies," Dmitri began, sounding hopeless.

Jenny followed the chattering group, hoping they wouldn't notice she was still blushing. She wasn't sure how it had happened, but in the last two years Caitlyn had gone from boss to friend, and that meant Jenny had been included in all their circles, and had seen some very odd things.

Being a member of the wedding party today, of all days—well, there was no way around it. It really—she hated to even think it—took the cake.

# Chapter 3

The Grand Hotel ballroom, where both the ceremony and reception would take place, looked like Jenny expected: breathtaking.

Masses of flowers, candles, silk tablecloths, white-jacketed waiters hurrying about, guests settling in their chairs . . . it was really kind of funny. A stranger to the wedding party could still easily see where to sit. All the staid, sober men and women in dark suits were on the groom's side, and all the cool, funky-looking people were on Stacy's side.

She stood with Caitlyn, who had a fixed smile on her face—Caitlyn really didn't like The Boss, for reasons Jenny had never quite been able to figure out. She assumed the guy gave lousy benefits or was stingy with vacation time. Not that Caitlyn ever had to work for him—she had Mag, the hottest salon in St. Paul.

Whatever the situation, it wasn't Jenny's business; Mag was Mag, and whatever Caitlyn did for The Boss was Caitlyn's business. Mostly she tried to keep her head down. Because when she didn't, fairly awful things happened. Well . . . the cake thing had turned out nicely. Still, the center of attention was no place for her. And this was no day for an awful thing.

The music droned on (she hated orchestral music . . . all that incessant violin screeching gave her a headache) as Stacy practically pranced down the aisle. She'd abandoned the colored contacts last year, and now her big, dark eyes sparkled. Her high cheekbones gave her the look of Egyptian royalty, and the low neckline gave her the look of royalty who was open to a good time.

Across the aisle, Dmitri was standing with The Boss, and that *was* a miracle. Dmitri hated The Boss, if possible, even more than Caitlyn did. And yet there he was, the best man! Oh, the things Stacy could do when she put her mind to it. Jenny was glad the bride was a friend, not an enemy.

Dmitri looked positively luscious, as usual; but The Boss was almost normal-looking, human even. He was short, but still had a couple of inches on Stacy. Not to mention a couple of years—he was in his forties. His most outstanding feature was his stature: his shoulders were powerfully built (Stacy had confided he needed all his suits custom-made).

In fact, The Boss always dressed well, usually in dark suits that were made so well you almost didn't notice them. Jenny reflected that he might be even better at blending into the background than she was. Did he not enjoy being the center of attention either, then?

His black hair was smoothed back—slicked back, really— so that his scalp resembled that of a seal. His eyebrows were pale, almost white. His eyes were the color of dirty ice. He was sleekly unobtrusive in a black suit and white dress shirt.

Caitlyn always said he looked like a mean egg, and Jenny had to agree. She certainly didn't know what had possessed Stacy to begin an affair with a much older, much scarier man, and then agree to marry him. Especially since Stacy had, as Caitlyn so exquisitely put it, "gone through more men than a cat through litter."

Love was weird.

And what did she call him during intimate moments? Surely not The Boss. Could it be? Maybe just an affectionate "Bossy." Or a reverent "Sir." If Stacy knew The Boss's real name, she wasn't telling. "Bossy"? Surely not.

Jenny suppressed a shudder. Another mystery for the ages. She tried desperately to get the mental image of their intimate moments out of her head. Caitlyn had the right idea.

She distracted herself by wondering, again, about the odd wedding group. Yes, she had seen a great many odd things in the last two years, not least of which was the fact that Caitlyn and Dmitri were very different from everyone else. The Boss (what could his real name be? Pete? Dave? Mark? John? Fred?) seemed to know all about it. Stacy, too. Jenny tried not to resent being kept in the dark, especially when it appeared to be cases involving government security, and, in fact, had found out a great deal on her own, but—

She wrenched her train of thought back to current events. The Boss's side was full of stiff men and women in suits; the family pew was conspicuously empty. Did The Boss have no family, then? She could relate.

On the other side, Stacy's folks were waving at her from the front row; as an old-school feminist, Stacy had not allowed her father to "give" her to The Boss, and had walked down the aisle alone. Jenny couldn't blame her. Fathers weren't much good to anybody. Fathers—

"Good afternoon," the minister began as Stacy and The Boss faced him. Then he coughed, or something coughed, in rapid succession, and then someone began to scream— maybe Stacy's mom—as The Boss toppled over into his bride, knocking her sprawling and getting blood all over her meringue wedding gown.

# Chapter 4

"Ambulances are on the way," Dmitri said.

"And your parents are helping the guests leave, hopefully without a stampede," Jenny added. Aside from a few screams, the filing-out had been relatively civilized. Rapid, but civilized.

"Move over, Stacy, I need to assess the damage," Dmitri ordered.

"You're speaking Russian, hon. Nobody can understand a word. Except me," Caitlyn added modestly. "Now *you* move, so *I* can assess."

Stacy looked up from where she was applying pressure and glared at both of them. "How could this have happened? *Again*? Weren't you scanning? Didn't you *see*?"

"Yes," Caitlyn grunted, trying to tug her friend away.

"And no," Dmitri said, ripping open The Boss's coat and vest.

"If you tickle me, Dmitri Novatur, I swear on your mother's shiny Baltic head I'll have you killed."

"My mother does not have a shiny head. He seems fine," Dmitri observed, and then he and Stacy glanced at Caitlyn.

She threw her hands up in a warding-off gesture. "I didn't

do it!" she practically screamed. "I swear I hate his fucking guts, but I didn't do this."

"Not her style," The Boss grunted. "Too subtle."

*Shot? Too subtle?* Jenny didn't comment, but had her doubts.

"I believe you; it's not your style, girlfriend. Ugh, someone help me get this thing off him. Oh, honey, how bad does it hurt? Did you crack a rib again?"

"Are *you* all right?" The Boss asked anxiously.

"I'm fine—and you still shouldn't have pushed me into the flower arrangements. Look at my hair!"

"Excuse me, can we get back to the freak at hand? Now that we've established you're not going to bleed out on the steps, I've gotta ask. Who wears a bulletproof vest on their wedding day?" Caitlyn snarked, though the answer seemed obvious enough to Jenny.

She wriggled in close—difficult, given all the people around him—and said, "Sir, shouldn't you be siccing the count and countess on the bad guys? It's only been about twenty-three seconds or so."

The Boss's gaze shifted to her and she shivered; it was like he could see all her secrets, and would keep them—for a price. "At least one of you is thinking."

"Blooow meee," Caitlyn sang.

"Mirage, Wolf, go bring me the bad guys. Any bad guys, really. Stacy, I'm fine, stop that annoying fussing. Jennifer, bring me the minister; I believe he's cowering someplace small—try the rest rooms. This wedding will resume in short order."

"Don't want to lose any of the deposits, huh, big guy?" Caitlyn asked sweetly.

"No, I'm determined to plough your best friend tonight as her husband, not her lover." Over Caitlyn's gags, The Boss added, "And somebody get this thing off me, it weighs a ton."

"Excuse me, Your Grace . . . Your Grace . . ."

"They're talking to you guys," Jenny said, because Caitlyn kept forgetting she was a countess. How did the EMTs know? Obviously, she answered her own question—they were in-house paras, workers for The Boss. Standing by? Was The Boss so meticulously detailed he made sure they were in the vicinity when he got married? That was a sobering thought. Meanwhile, the EMTs were fighting to get into the inner circle.

"Let's go," Caitlyn said, "before they keep going with the 'Your Grace' stuff."

"Well," Dmitri said reasonably, following her out the door at what looked like a brisk trot, but was really much faster, "you *did* marry a count."

Over the protests of the medics, and in compliance with The Boss's terse orders, Stacy helped him out of the vest, which was several ounces heavier with the lead acquisition, and he sat up with a gasp. Several gasps, actually; he was pale with pain.

"Once again, death whispers in my ear." He was speaking with difficulty, his pupils the size of pinpricks from shock. "And once again, you chase him away."

"Spare me. I'm just glad you're okay. Can't we even get married without scary shit like this happening?" Stacy wept a little and Jenny backed away, figuring it was as good a time as any to find the minister.

"We *will* get married today, Stacy. And stay married for a long time. I promised you the night we got engaged."

"But if something happens to you—"

"Something is always happening to me. That's the business we're in. You should know, darling—you're pre-law. Some day you'll have more enemies than I."

She buried her face in her hands and he patted her gently, soothingly. "You're an asshole," she sobbed.

"You're a tart. Help me up."

"Not 'til the minister comes back. You can rest until then, at the very least."

Hurrying away to do her duty, Jenny was conflicted. She was a little afraid of The Boss, and thought Stacy was too loud, with all her emotions . . . *out there*. But right now, she was quite jealous of both of them.

# Chapter 5

She found the minister in the men's room. He was trying to talk the bad guy into giving up his gun. Their voices were bouncing off the tile, and Jenny had just enough time to wish she'd knocked, but then it was too late, and she was standing under bright fluorescents and thinking, *This is the cleanest men's room I've ever seen. Also, the third men's room I've ever seen.*

"Don't you think you should have planned this better?" she asked because, honestly, it was the first thought that popped into her head.

Not: *Help!*

Not: *Oh my God, he's got a gun!*

The bad guy grinned at her. He was dressed, to her disappointment, like most bad guys: neck to ankles in black fatigues, and fairly bristling with guns and knives and armor. His hair was cut brutally short—no more than a dark brown fuzz covered his skull. His dark eyes almost disappeared into laugh lines while he smiled at her, but she could see they were tipped at the ends, not quite almond-shaped, giving him an exotic look. It was a little like being in the men's room with a panther. Though without a firmer frame of reference, she probably couldn't be sure.

"I planned things just fine, sweetie," he informed her in a North Carolina accent. *Ah planned things jest fahn, sweetie.* "Is he dead?"

To add the final touch of weirdness to the day, the bad guy pulled out a spork from nowhere and nibbled on the end.

A spork? But the nearest KFC was—

She wrenched her thoughts back to a logical track. Sporks be damned. Time to focus. Caitlyn and Dmitri were somewhere else in the building. The Boss was probably in an ambulance by now. Stacy was a civilian. The minister probably wasn't armed. All the urinals were empty. It was up to her.

"Hmm mmm hmm hmm," she replied.

"What?" he said, taking a step toward her, putting the spork back into his bad-guy Bat belt.

She wrung her hands and moved closer. "Don't hurt us, please! I'll tell you where he is, only mmm hmm mmm."

"Don't be scared, honey." *Don't be scayed, honeh.* She fought the mad impulse to giggle. It was a little like talking to Foghorn Leghorn, in Kevlar. "Now what's that?"

She threw her bouquet in his face, poor thing that it was after she'd denuded it to make the cake. He flinched back and she clawed for the pistol in the shoulder holster, ducking as he swung at her with almost no force. What was that— was he really not trying to hurt her? Moron.

*(You'd better be sure, if you try for a man's gun,)*

She was sure. The Velcro tore . . .

*(if he's any good he'll have one in the chamber, one in the chamber, one in the chamber)*

. . . and she had the gun. She stuck it in his face the moment he cut his losses and backed up.

"You'd better come with me," she said.

"Oh, dear God," the minister said. He was in the far corner. Praying, not swearing. Funny. Half an hour ago, the guy had looked like he was in his early thirties. Now he looked ready for a retirement home. The black, of course, didn't help.

The bad guy hadn't lost his smile through the whole thing (weird!), and now he held his rifle out in front of him like a peace offering to a god, carefully put it down, backed up more, and raised his hands. "You got me, honey. I'll come quietly."

"Oh."

He laughed. A great laugh, booming and rich. It echoed off the tiles. "You sound disappointed, honey! Were you hoping for a smackdown in the boys' room?"

"Never you mind." She moved to the side, the gun never wavering; she had sighted on the middle of his forehead. "Let's go, Carolina."

"Aww. Who told you mah nickname?"

# Chapter 6

Kevin Stone felt abnormally cheerful as the gorgeous blonde escorted him to a conference room on the north side of the hotel. He should have been plenty pissed, not to mention scared for his life, but hell, she was so damn cute, and quick, too.

He was pretty sure he could have stopped her from taking his side arm, but he would have had to break her arm in a couple of places, or possibly her nose; and hell, it was too nice a day to go around roughing up the ladies.

And her nose was way too cute to break.

He was a little disappointed to see The Boss waiting for him in the conference room, gray-faced but still alive. Aw, who was he kidding? If he'd really wanted The Boss dead, he would have gone for a head shot.

No cops, which he expected—The Boss liked to keep things tidy and in-house.

The guests were long gone, which was a surprise. The rubberneck factor was usually pretty high. People lost all sense once they got over the initial duck-and-cover impulse. He imagined O.S.I. personnel had been firm about clearing the perimeter.

Mirage and The Wolf were there as well, and the three of

them looked shocked. Not to see him, of course. To see the cute little receptionist holding his Glock.

"We got your call," The Boss said, staring. "I sent the paramedics away. Nothing broken."

"That's good," the cutie replied. Not that Mirage was hard on the eyes, either—with those long legs, sky-blue eyes, and white-blond hair, she was really something—but she was taken. Big-time taken. By the fellow standing to her right, and Kevin had about sixty other more important things to do than get into a pissing match with The Wolf over a woman. "Uh, while you were doing that, I went and caught the bad guy for you." She seemed to gesture with the gun as if to say, *here he is*.

The Boss blinked. Mirage and The Wolf looked at each other. Nobody said anything. Kevin stifled a laugh.

"I, uh, don't have the authority to arrest anyone. So I thought you should, uh, take him into custody? Or what-ever."

"They can't arrest me either, honey," he told her, nib-bling on a fresh spork. It wasn't really a laughing matter, but damn, the feeling was fine. And there had been goddamned little to laugh about these last four years. Six. Twenty. "Isn't that right, Big Boss? The O.S.I. can't arrest me. And all's *you* can do is send me out without enough intel and get me killed. That's what you do, right?"

"Who *are* you?" Mirage asked. "And if you really wanted him dead, here's some friendly advice—next time try a head shot."

His ego jumped up and he couldn't keep his mouth shut. "Honey, if I wanted him dead, he'd be in a rubber bag in the morgue."

"Don't tease me," she whispered.

"And—you shot him but did not want him dead?" The Wolf asked.

"Stacy was the target," The Boss corrected, almost absently. "Not me."

"Stacy was *what?*" Mirage had started calmly enough, but the last word was pretty much shrieked. Kevin was surprised the water glasses on the table didn't shatter. Oooh, Blondie had a temper. Her fist dropped to the table and broke off a chunk like the thing was made of cardboard. "Chum, you'd better start talking."

"Yes, you'd really better," the cutie with the gun said, sounding almost apologetic. "Because that's going to be a much bigger problem for us. Everybody's much fonder of Stacy than her fiancé." She glanced at The Boss. "No offense."

The Boss inclined his head. "None taken."

"Gonna be a long story," he said cheerfully, fishing for a fresh spork. "You ladies better get comfortable."

# Chapter 7

After an impersonal but thorough frisking by The Wolf, Kevin was seated at one end of the table. The cutie popped the clip on his Glock, hit the slide, and caught the round in the chamber as it popped out. Then she set it by the pile of weapons Kevin had brought to the wedding.

"We've got some questions," The Boss began. Then he cut his gaze to the cutie. "And I've got a few for you, too, dear, but time enough for that later."

The cutie shrugged and looked down at her hands, then back at the pile of guns and knives and flash grenades.

"You don't know me? You don't recognize me?" Kevin asked him pleasantly. His temper, a vicious animal that he kept in a too-small cage, stirred. "You sure, Boss?"

"I'm sure."

"Pretty sure?"

"Positively sure."

"My name's Kevin Stone. I work for the C.O.P. I've been undercover the last four years."

"If that's true, then you know General Bracton."

"Brac's dead."

"Undercover," The Wolf interrupted quietly, "doing what?"

"Infiltrating a splinter cell down south. Sort of the O.S.I.'s opposite number. Y'all do something good, they do something bad. Y'all use your funding to make helpful robot killers, they use theirs to blow up banks and pick up the pieces to put in their purse. They call themselves S.T.A.R.—Support Tracking and Recon. We call 'em the Snakepit."

"Four years in the Snakepit?" The Wolf clarified.

"Yup, are you getting it now? Or do I need to talk slower?"

"We, ah, get it, as you say, but there's a problem."

Kevin snorted. "Only one?"

"C.O.P. lost their funding nineteen months ago," The Boss said abruptly, with the air of a man who wants to deliver the bad news quickly and get it over with. "It's been shut down."

"Probably because the Senate didn't know who the hell they were. O.S.I.? C.O.P.? S.T.A.R.? Come on," Caitlyn said, "it's like alphabet soup from hell."

"Ah-yup, I figured when nobody was returning my calls." His temper was rattling the bars now—it wanted out, it wanted to do some damage, it wanted to be free. *Out, let it out.* But he kept his voice nice and light. Training, it seemed, was good for more than hitting the bull's eye.

"They forgot about you?" the cutie asked. "And didn't pull you out first?" She gave a small shake of her head, looking small and pretty in her bridesmaid's gown.

"We all know the risks in this sort of work, Jenny." But Mirage's eyes sobered with a certain respect as she reconsidered him. "No wonder you carry around three guns."

*Four, honey.* "That's not why I came here," he said. "I'm here because the Snakepit's the only place paying me now. They gave me a new assignment—shoot The Boss's pretty little bride-to-be. And—"

*I couldn't do it. Not even to stay safe. Not even to keep my hid-*

*ing place. Couldn't shoot a woman, a civilian, in cold blood. Nope. And nope and nope.*

"—and saw your chance for revenge!" Jenny struggled between understanding and loathing. "Hitting Stacy did nothing for you. But hitting him—that would make you feel better, and it would probably satisfy the Snakepit, since hurting him would hurt her. You could always say you missed, or he saw you and put himself in front of his fiancée."

*No.* Kevin shrugged. "Yeah, sure. That's how it was."

The Wolf was scanning him with those little freak teeny robots-nanobytes. Mirage, he saw, didn't bother. That was interesting.

"Is there more to the story, Mr. Stone?" The Wolf asked, just as cool as a naked baby in February.

"Yeah, there's more. I want to go to a fucking—er, a safe house and be debriefed. And I want a shower and I want a Big Mac. And I want a fu—an apology from the government of the U.S. of A. for dumping me in the Snakepit and then forgetting about me. One from The Boss here might be nice, too."

There was a long, awkward silence when everyone looked everywhere but at Kevin.

"It's okay," the cutie said at last. "You can say *fucking*. We don't mind."

"I's raised," he replied, trying not to smile at her earnest-ness, "not to swear around the ladies. My daddy would beat me raw, he heard me talking to you like that. But that's good to know, Miss—"

"Branch. Jennifer Branch." She tilted her head slightly in greeting. Perhaps she already knew he had a fourth gun.

"You got quick hands, Miss Branch."

"Well." She shrugged. "I'm a receptionist."

"For him?"

"Gosh, no!" She laughed. "I work in a hair salon." She pointed to Mirage. "Her salon."

"Yeah, nobody here works for The Boss," Mirage said quickly. "It's almost like you're among friends."

"I gotta see that hair salon," he replied, and for some reason that made *both* the ladies smile.

# Chapter 8

"Everything checks out—prints, everything. He is who he says he is. Not," The Boss added in a mutter, "that finding his files was easy."

"Um." Caitlyn cleared her throat. "Can we wait a second before we get back into this? No offense, Jen, but what are you still doing here? This is sort of, uh, Boss business."

It was later that same night; the minister had performed a quickie ceremony and The Boss had sent his new bride to the honeymoon suite with an escort of seven armed guards. Stacy had gone, cursing and protesting the whole way. Jenny was a little surprised she herself had not been escorted out with the bride.

Meanwhile, The Boss's many minions had taken Kevin into protective custody, printing him, debriefing him, and bringing him fast food. Where this was happening exactly, of course, Jennifer had no idea.

And here they were, back in that same conference ballroom, The Boss popping Darvocets like they were Tic Tacs, and everybody feeling less than fresh.

"I'd like her to stay," The Boss said, which Jenny found surprising; she had started to get up to leave.

"But—"

"Caitlyn, she's earned the right to stay. Unless it was really one of you two who brought me the shooter, disguised as a salon secretary in a blond wig? No? As I guessed. Then may I continue?"

"Stone could have aimed about a foot lower," she muttered, slumping in her chair, "and spilled your brains."

"Singular wit. As I was saying, he is who he says he is. What are our options?"

"First things first," Dmitri said with palm raised. "Did we really dump him and forget about him?"

"The C.O.P.s did, yes."

"But it's all the same thing, right? We're all working for the same government. I mean, you and he are. We don't, uh, work for you."

"How could such a thing have happened?" Dmitri asked, ignoring Caitlyn's interruption.

"He was deep in," The Boss answered placidly. "For weeks after the budget cuts were announced, there was no way to warn him. By the time we tried, he had disappeared. He was either dead, a double agent, or deeper than ever. No matter what the reason, we had to cut the connection. Agents are trained to find their way back, under such circumstances."

"And he did. Eventually. Are there others?"

"We're working on it. I would like to think he was the only one." Nobody was sure whether The Boss liked to think that because it was distasteful to leave an undercover agent in the field, or because he didn't have the patience for more bullets today.

"Well." Caitlyn looked around the small room. "Okay, that's pretty bad, but at least he's out and done now, right?"

"Hmm."

"You'd like him to go back in," Jenny guessed.

"What?" Caitlyn cried.

"Of course they do," Dmitri added. "It's the only logical course of action."

"*Why?*"

"To finish the job."

"What job? C.O.P. doesn't exist anymore—ergo, there is no job."

"There's always work, I bet."

"Correct, Jennifer. My, my, but don't you have a knack for this sort of thing." The Boss eased back in his chair, wincing as he felt his ribs. He let out a breath, then said, "However did you get his gun away from him?"

"Because he let me."

"Is that right? Hmm . . ."

"Dude."

"Yes, Caitlyn?"

"Dude. No."

"Calm down. We've all had enough of your annoying hysterics for one day."

"Watch yourself, sir," Dmitri said, narrowing his eyes.

Caitlyn didn't even notice. "*Dude. No.* You've contaminated my best friend—thanks to you, she had the bad guys trying to shoot her, and worse, you married her an hour ago! All that is bad enough; you are *not* sucking Jenny into the O.S.I. Not only is she a great friend, she's the best receptionist I've ever had."

"Well," Jenny allowed, blushing at all the kind words, "I *am* the only one who knows the new phone system."

"Right!" Caitlyn pounced on that fact like a tiger on a raw steak. "So you can't have her." Caitlyn jabbed a thumb at her own chest. "She's *mine*."

"Really, Caitlyn, you're so paranoid."

"People really are out to get me," she replied flatly, "and that's a fact. You're plotting against me, and that's also a fact."

"True enough. Back to business. As I was trying to explain, I discussed the matter with my superior and they'd like Mr. Stone to go back undercover."

"Does your superior have a forked tail and horns?"

Ignoring Caitlyn, he continued. "Apparently the Snakepit does quite a lot of damage and he's still in a unique position to infiltrate and disrupt their doings."

"Yeah, well, it's kind of moot, right? You can't ask him. The guy's been living with the enemy for four years, probably scared shitless half the time, wondering what he'd done to get dumped in with the bad guys, and now that he's out, you can't ask him to go back."

"*Can't* is relative, dear."

There was a pause while Caitlyn digested that, while Jenny glanced at Dmitri—oh, yes, he could see where this was going. It wasn't difficult to surmise, really. The real difficulty . . . well . . .

She had an unkind thought for her boss and friend, something Stacy had once said in jest: *With Caitlyn, everything takes twelve seconds longer.*

Meanwhile, the yelling had recommenced. "You aren't *really* thinking about *asking* him, right? Not really? Oh, look who I'm talking to; you've got the conscience of a wood tick. Of *course* you're gonna ask him—poor guy finally gets out and now you're gonna ask him to go back to hell. Without his Big Macs, I bet."

"No," The Boss replied. "We aren't going to ask him." He glanced at Jenny, who had already braced herself for the rest of it. "Jennifer is."

# Chapter 9

As expected, Mirage and The Wolf were knocking on his door (not "his" door, but rather the safe house door—so really, the taxpayers' door; but he was the one who had to answer it) before the clock struck nine.

The surprise was, they'd brought the receptionist cutie with them.

"Thanks again," Mirage said, shaking his hand, "for shooting that jerk."

"Aw," he drawled, "'twazn't nothin', ma'am."

The cutie giggled at that, and shook his hand also. The Wolf closed the door behind them (they had, presumably, been vetted by the two checkpoints and the four security guards) and held out his hand. Curious, Kevin seized it and shook. Hard. How strong was this guy, anyway? Surely those itty-bitty robots in his bloodstream couldn't account for all that—

The bones in his hands ground together as The Wolf squeezed back. "Nice to see you again," Kevin said, almost gasped. Damn! His daddy said you could tell a real man by the strength of his handshake and if that was true, The Wolf was the realest man on the planet. He managed to wrest free, and squashed the urge to massage his throbbing fingers. Speaking of squashed, he was almost afraid to look at his hand. "Come on in and grab a chair."

"We're sorry to bother you," the cutie—Jennifer—said. "Ah." She stopped.

He could see why. He was in custody; he was the bad guy. He'd shot the groom. But they were coming to ask a favor, treating him like a colleague—which he also was. So it was hard to figure out which way to go: soft or hard.

Since Jennifer was there, he figured soft. He should have been angry, should have let the beast loose. But he was so damn glad to see her again . . .

"Don't sweat it. The fridge is empty, but I could ask the guards to rustle somethin' up, if you're hungry."

"No, we're fine." Mirage was looking around the small living room, at the McDonalds' bags wadded in the garbage, at the plasma screen which was running CNN and a stream of data across the bottom. Anywhere but at him, he noticed.

She must be, he thought, new at the game. To be embarrassed still. Or at least, to show it.

"So what can I do for the O.S.I.?" he asked, figuring they might as well get to it.

"There's no easy way to say this," Jennifer began, "so I'm just going to say it. They'd like you to go back. To that, er, Snakepit."

"Ah-yup. And do *they* have some sort of plan so I don't die?"

"Sure!" Mirage said heartily. "There's a plan. Of course there's a plan! And it's a big plan, too. Oh, the plan they have!"

"Can I get you a shovel for all that bullshit?"

Color rose in her cheeks and she looked away. "Uh, no thanks, I'm fine."

"And they sent the receptionist here to soften me up?"

"Hey," Mirage said, offended. "She's a business manager."

"Who answers the phones. Yes. I think—" She looked around the room and raised her hands, palms up, for a moment. "I think The Boss has plans for me."

"And we're here because we wouldn't let her come alone."

"Honey, I'm *sure* The Boss has plans for you." That was how the guy operated; if he couldn't recruit you into the O.S.I. by playing the patriot card, or suck you in with your own curiosity, he'd outright kidnap you as an indentured servant. "Just like he's got plans for all of us. Now: what are you gonna do when I tell you no, I ain't going back?"

"I'd tell you to drop the act and do what you're dying to do anyway?" she guessed.

"Way to soften him up," Mirage muttered, looking relieved when he laughed.

"Are we just gonna stand around in this crappy living room all night?" he asked. "Or are you bums gonna take me out and buy me a drink?"

*The Bucket*
*1st Avenue, Minneapolis*
*Three hours later*

"Kevin! Watch this!"

He groaned. "Come on, Caitlyn."

"Are you watching?" She steadied herself on the edge of the bar and almost—but not quite—tipped over. "You're not watching."

"I'm watching, Crissake."

"She has issues with authority," Jennifer told him. "She alternately resents it, and craves attention from it."

"Great." Louder, so she could hear him from their table. "I'm watching, go ahead."

Caitlyn finished the last of her margarita (peach) and hurled darts across the room too quickly for his vision to track. They seemed to sprout from the center of the dartboard all at once, like a magician's trick.

"Ha-hah! I told you I could do three at a time."

"Yeah, you're a fu—a genius," Kevin said. A drunken, nutty genius with baby robots in her bloodstream that made her deadly even when she couldn't hardly stand up. *Your tax dollars at work, ladies and gentlemen.* "Have another drink."

"Don't mind if I do." Caitlyn plopped back in her chair and signaled the harried waitress. "You know, ever since my accident it takes a lot to get me drunk. But I think I'm managing nicely."

"That's your ninth margarita. If you weren't so perky, I'd call an ambulance."

"Oh, well." She shrugged and nearly fell off the chair. "I've got a really great metagonism. Mantabonistic. Megabogibbin."

"Metabolism," Jenny suggested.

"No, that's not it. You're just making up drunk words, Jenny."

"The Boss'd choke you like a rat, he saw you doing all that stuff in public."

"Really?" She seemed pleased by the idea. "Think he'd be pissed? Think he'd fire me? Not that he can, because—hic!—I don't work for him." Then she looked around. "Where's Dmitri?"

"I'm right here, dear."

She jumped and nearly spilled her drink, which the waitress had just set down. "There you are. Don't sneak like that. You're always *sneaking*."

"Sorry." He eyed her drink. "I'm surprised the waitress hasn't cut you off."

"In this place?" Kevin snorted. "Y'all could strip and set your butts on fire, and the booze would keep on coming."

"What a charming thought," The Wolf commented.

"Friday night on the Ave, friends and neighbors."

Jennifer sipped her cherry Coke. "You brought us here to drink, and you're not drinking."

He didn't touch his ice water. "Oh, you know. Just wanted to get out of there for a while more'n anything else." *And see if you're real people behind those bland government faces. And talk to you some more, blue-eyes.*

"It must be sweet to be out."

Actually, it was nerve-wracking. He'd been under so long, he wasn't sure he knew how to be Kevin Stone again. He changed the subject.

"Him, I know why he's not drinking, he's decided he's on point. How 'bout you, sunshine? Nothing in your Coke but grenadine—how come?"

She shrugged and smiled vaguely. "Designated driver."

*Lie.*

"Cuz I'm buyin', honey, if you're, you know, a little light in the pocketbook."

"No, it's fine."

"Yeah," Caitlyn said, and belched lightly against the back of her hand. The nails, Kevin noticed, were talon-long and painted dark pink. "So drop it, bud."

"Sorry," he said. "Didn't mean to get anybody's hair up."

"It's fine," Jenny said, still smiling that odd smile.

"Yeah, s'fine, so butt out," Caitlyn slurred.

"Caitlyn. It's fine."

"Yup, everything's fine," Kevin agreed, wondering about the tension. Funny thing, the tension wasn't coming from Jenny, but from her pal. Caitlyn had the protective instincts of a grizzly.

"Quite," The Wolf said.

Kevin searched for a fresh spork, failed, rooted around some more, gave up. "So, what? What's up next?"

"That's up to you," The Wolf pointed out.

"Is it?" he said, looking at Jenny.

Caitlyn yawned. "So, when y'gonna make up your mind?"

"Maybe tomorrow. Maybe next month."

"No one would blame you if you didn't want to go back in," Jenny said.

*I'd blame me.* "Thanks."

"Do you want a ride back to the safe house?" Jenny asked.

"I'd love one, sugar."

"I better not drive," Caitlyn said, "but Dmitri can get the car—"

"—and drop us off," Jenny finished.

"Us?" Caitlyn asked.

"Us?" Kevin asked.

# Chapter 10

"So." Jenny had looked at all the bookshelves (stocked with Dan Brown paperbacks and back issues of Oprah), poked around the near-empty kitchen, and examined the DVD collection (all the Harry Potter movies, *Gladiator*, the Austin Powers collection, and every Superman movie). "You know, this looks a lot like—I don't know."

"Yeah, they can't quite get it right. It gives off cheap-hotel vibes, even if it's supposed to be a house. Not lived-in enough."

"Or only lived in by strangers passing through," she said absently, flipping through *Angels and Demons*.

"Yup. Get you anything?"

"No, thank you."

"No booze or anything . . . how about some O.J.?"

"No, thank you."

He plunked down on the couch. "So, what? What'd you come back for?"

She glanced at him, chewing on her lower lip. "I don't know. I guess—I guess I wasn't ready to go back to my life yet."

"Tell me about it."

She laughed.

"So, tell me about yourself."

"You first."

"Aw, it's boring."

Her gaze sharpened. "Sure."

"Naw, it is."

"Well, my life story is a tiresome tale as well."

"So."

"So," she replied.

"So we're both pretty dull, then?"

"Yup," she said, aping his accent.

"You don't wanna tell me one thing about yourself?"

"Not especially. But I'm kind of wondering what led you to the Snakepit."

"Well, I'll tell you what. Let's trade. I'll give you something and you return the favor."

She fluttered her eyelashes. "Why, I hardly know what to say."

"That sounds like a 'no' to me."

She shrugged.

"Tell you what." He tried to think of something. And it came to him while he was glancing around the room and saw the magazine rack, which was filled with games instead of magazines. "Play you for it."

Her eyebrows, pale yellow against the perfect cream of her skin, arched. "Really? Play what?"

"Go Fish?" she said again.

He shrugged apologetically. They were sitting, knees together, around the small coffee table in the living room. "Sorry. Couldn't find any poker chips."

"I s'pose Monopoly was out of the question."

"I hate that game. It's so boring."

"Unlike the intellectually stimulating Go Fish."

"Aw, hush up and look at your cards."

She smiled in spite of herself, and picked up her hand.

"Okay," he was saying, "so we're clear on the rules. If you don't got the card you need, you can draw or you can talk. Okay?"

"Okay."

"You got any fours?"

"Go fish," she said gravely.

He hesitated, then said, "Okay, I'll get this going. I got into the Snakepit to get away from my family. The bad guys."

She digested that, then said, "Do you have any sixes?"

He put one down.

*Nuts.*

"Do you have any nines?"

"Go fish."

He scowled. "This ain't hardly fair. I'm doing all the talking."

"You picked the game."

"Well, I'm gonna draw." He picked up several cards until he finally put down the nine of hearts. "Got any queens?"

She started to reach for the pile, nibbled her lip, then said, "My parents were alcoholics."

His eyes were on his cards. "Yup, I figured."

"Do you have any aces?"

He put one down. "You got any queens?"

"You know I—" Hmm. Irritating man. And damned if she was going to cop out by reaching for new cards. On the other hand, she wasn't in the mood for *This Is Your Life*, either.

So she put her cards down, and pulled her tee-shirt over her head.

"Whoa!"

"So, I changed the rules."

"We're playing strip Go Fish?"

"We are now."

"Aw, hell. Uh—not that I don't like your little bra there, but the point of this was to find out about each other."

"Well," she said reasonably, "now you've found out I like peach."

"Umm," he said. "You got any queens?"

"I think it's my turn. Do you have any jacks?"

He put down his hand, reached down, and pulled off a sock.

"Now who isn't talking?" she teased.

"Hey, you changed the rules. You got any queens?"

She stood, unzipped her pants, kicked out of them. Of all the nights to go sockless! "Do you have any jacks?"

He pulled off the other sock. "You got any threes?"

She laid down a three. "Do you have any threes?"

He started to pull his shirt over his head, hesitated, then said, "They were *bad* bad guys. I mean, they weren't good at it. So on top of not wanting to be in the mob, it was embarrassing to be in a family of screwups." Pause. "You got any kings?"

She looked at him for what seemed, to her, to be a long time. Finally, she said, "My parents aren't around anymore."

"I'm sorry," he said.

"It's stupid, the whole thing was stupid. They could have done things so differently. Do you have any kings?"

He took off his shirt. She tried not to stare at the broadly muscled chest, the scars. His lips were moving. Was he talking to her? It was hard to hear over the roaring in her ears.

"Sorry?"

"You got any twos?"

As a matter of fact, she did. As a further matter of fact, she was in it now, and decided to just suck it up, the way a kid got rid of too much Halloween candy on November first. "They were both alcoholics—except in those days you called them drunks. And they hooked up in what I suppose was a very natural way—at every party they were the two drunkest people there."

He kept his eyes on his cards. That made it easier, somehow. She wasn't sure she could have borne his gaze. Bad enough she was barefoot, and shirtless, with a hand full of twos and queens.

"They'd finish up every party together and then hit the bars. They'd close the bars and go to their apartments and finish a six-pack. My dad would," she added thoughtfully. "My mom's drink of choice was the screwdriver. You know how most kids associate their moms with good smells, like chocolate chip cookies or meatloaf or whatever? If I get a whiff of Gray Goose, I get misty."

"Me, too, but for different reasons."

She smiled at his poor joke. "Do you have any fours?"

He laid down a four. "You got any queens?"

She stared at the queen of clubs and continued. "You know how it is when you're drunk—everybody's nicer, more attractive. You tell people things you'd normally keep quiet about. And they built this sort of—this false intimacy. They thought it was love.

"By the time my mom sobered up and left the party, she had a four-year-old child in a three-year-old marriage. Only problem was, my dad *never* wanted to leave the party. So she did A.A. by herself and, later, we both did Al-Anon. She went back to college, got her law degree, got a terrific new job clerking for a local judge, and then, of course, her liver gave out on her and she died before she could get a new one. And I was left with my dad."

He put his cards down. All pretense of a game was gone. "How old were you when she died?"

"Twelve."

"But I thought you said your mama decorated cakes for her job."

"She used to—it was the perfect job. Show up a few nights a week, sample the wine while you're on break, and use your late mornings to drink."

"And your daddy?"

"My dad what?"

"What'd he do?"

"He's in sales."

"He's still alive?"

"Sure. Do you have any fives?"

"My brothers are the biggest screwups in the world," he said. "Bigger than my dad, even. And that's saying something. They've been shot at more than me, and that's saying something, too. It's a miracle any of them are still alive. Shoot, if my little brother wasn't in prison, he'd prob'ly be dead. D'you have any aces?"

"My dad's still in the house I grew up in. Still drives the same car he bought when I was just a kid. Believe me, we were both counting the days until I left for college. He did not take my mom's death well, I can assure you." She laughed, a bitter giggle that hurt her throat. "No, he didn't care for being a single dad one bit."

She saw the cards crumple in his grip. "He smack you around a little bit, hon?"

"Oh, no! Much worse. He just didn't give a shit. I was extremely unimportant in the scheme of things, and he made sure I knew it. Some daughters have fathers who leave them for good one day. I had a father who left me for good, every day of my life. I wish he had hit me, or really took off. But he came back just often enough to kill another piece of my childhood. That's all he did, I guess." She laid down her cards, showing him the queens and the fours and the twos and the jacks.

He glanced down, then back up. "My daddy used to say a poor dad's better than none at all."

"My daddy never said much of anything besides what a useless little bitch I was," she replied, and that pretty much closed out the evening for the both of them.

# Chapter 11

"Assuming I agree to your request—"

"Think of it more like an order," The Boss said mildly.

"—what makes you think I can get back in the pit?"

"Why would you even want to?" Caitlyn asked, drumming her fingers on the desk in front of her.

They all looked at her, and she colored defensively. "Look, the guy's been out on a limb for—what? Four years? How come he's even considering going back? He's out. He's done. Am I the only one who has trouble with this?"

The Boss nodded at Jenny, who almost did some blushing of her own. But, like a good pupil called upon, she answered. "He's considering it because the Snakepit is up to something."

"They're always up to something," Kevin said glumly.

"And Mr. Stone still has a conscience. He can't just sit by, knowing what he knows, and wait for the bombs to drop, or whatever."

"*Lieutenant* Stone," Kevin corrected her with a wink.

"Lieutenant, then." She took a nervous sip of her (excellent) coffee and tried not to stare back at him. God, he was just so *great*-looking; what was it about men in uniform? Maybe it was just him—the dark fatigues made him look lean and strong, the bristling weaponry made him look dangerous, the smile made him look charming.

To distract herself, she looked around the office again. Jennifer had never been to O.S.I. and couldn't get over how much like a regular company it looked. Cubes, computers, administrative assistants, clerks, cafeteria workers, conference rooms, restrooms, emergency exits, stairwells, fancy elevators, and executive suites.

"You're pretty sharp," he added.

"No, I'm not," she corrected, almost sharply. "Everybody in the room knows this. It's just, Caitlyn goes out of her way not to be involved. So by comparison, I look really smart."

Caitlyn opened her mouth but, at a look from her husband, closed it.

"Uh," Kevin said, and then *he* closed *his* mouth.

Caitlyn and Dmitri had brought her straight to The Boss's office on the tenth floor with no fuss and no fanfare: she hadn't even had to show her I.D. It was something to consider; her friends had some rank, for sure.

Although, if pressed, they would both deny working for The Boss; it was certainly no secret how much they disliked him.

Like him or not, the fact was that they both periodically disappeared, sometimes for weeks at a time, sometimes apart, more often together. "Vacations," Caitlyn would explain it away nervously when she asked Jenny to look after the salon.

But nobody—Jenny didn't care how much money they had—nobody took that many vacations. The fact that Caitlyn remained in denial about her status was irrelevant.

The Boss's office was like any CEO's—all dark leather and wood, with a formal outer office for an assistant (a pleasant red-headed woman named Sharon, with as many freckles as IQ points—a formidable thought).

"Jennifer—stop scaring me."

"I'm sorry?" she asked, startled.

"What are you, some kind of super-genius? I mean, I know you're smart, obviously you're smart, but this is just weird. You're around people who do heads, so you pick up style tips, and now you're around, uh, people in government work, and now you're figuring out all this—uh—"

"Spy stuff?" she asked. "It's all right, Caitlyn. I figured it out a few months ago. For heaven's sake. I'd have to be pretty dumb not to."

"Yeah, it's all right," Kevin yawned, propping his booted feet up on The Boss's desk. "I like 'em brainy."

"She's a chameleon personality," Dmitri explained. "It's a typical condition found in Generation X'ers."

"You're a Gen X'er," Caitlyn pointed out. "*I'm* a Gen X'er. *We're all Gen X'ers.*"

"Barely," Dmitri sniffed.

"That's a psychological theory that hasn't been definitely proven," Jenny felt obliged to mention.

"What is?" Caitlyn asked.

"Successful Gen X'ers are, to quote Dr. Rosen on the subject—"

"Can I take my nap now?"

"—'are tormented by anxiety, fear of failure, and a lack of control over the forces that affect their lives.'"

"So?" Caitlyn asked. "Welcome to the world."

"'To cope,'" Dmitri continued, ignoring his wife, "'many have adopted "chameleon" personalities, pretending to be what others want them to be . . .'"

"I resent that," Caitlyn said.

"It's not all about you, dear," The Boss replied a little sharply.

"And—and that's basically all there is on that," Dmitri finished, somewhat abruptly. Jennifer said nothing, though she knew he had skipped the part about how chameleon-ism was basically self-defeating, and the cost was very high, emotionally.

*Oh, and also, over time, pretending to be what you're not be-comes permanent. Crazy, much? Like father, like daugh—*

"I apologize," Dmitri was saying, "for getting us off topic."

"That's all right," Caitlyn said, leaning over and giving his knee a smack. "I do it all the time."

"Well, well," Kevin said, an admiring look on his face. His brown eyes twinkled at her. "No wonder you're the hot commodity 'round these parts."

Jenny felt herself blushing again, and silently cursed. Bad enough to be a boring pale blonde living in Minnesota, with the *de rigueur* blue eyes and long hair, but her com-plexion was always a dead giveaway to her emotional state.

"Be that as it may," The Boss said, forcing them back on track, "we were discussing how Kevin might reinfiltrate the Snakepit."

"Assuming he goes," Caitlyn added. "*That's* what we were discussing."

"How nice." The Boss gave her a wintry smile. "You were paying attention. Allow me to make note of the date and time. Also, Lieutenant, if you don't get your feet off my desk, you'll spend the rest of your life wondering which Big Mac is laced with poison."

Jenny almost laughed as Kevin sat up so straight, so quickly, he almost toppled out of his chair. "You leave the McDonalds Corporation alone," he warned.

"Dude! Didn't you see Super Size Me?"

"We don't all have efficient little baby robots cutting the fat out of our bloodstream every minute," Kevin practically snapped.

"Nobody's taking away your Big Macs," Jenny soothed. "That would be cruel and unusual." She herself was partial to the Filet-O-Fish.

"Goddamned right," he grumped. "But getting back to what we were jawin' about, you guys are giving me too much credit. The guys in the Pit'll shoot me on sight."

"Not if you bring them something they want."

"I can't explain going off the grid for almost twenty-four hours, not to mention coming back empty-handed."

"I can circulate arrest paperwork," The Boss said.

"So anyone hacking on him would think he was lawfully detained?" Dmitri asked.

"Exactly."

"And then he—what? Escaped? Was bailed out? By whom?"

"An escape, I think," The Boss replied. "Perhaps in transit."

"And he's bringing back—what?"

"Information."

"Discs, paperwork, what? And how did he get it?"

"He could bring *me* back," Jennifer suggested, and smiled through the expected uproar.

# Chapter 12

"It's a tremendously daring idea," The Boss said.

"Shut up," Caitlyn snapped. "Jenny, listen to reason. You're a receptionist, not a spy. This is not a movie, it's not television. This shit is an excellent way to get your head blown off. I don't even work here, and I've lost count of how many times I've been shot at."

"She's right," Kevin piped up helpfully. "I've almost had my head blown off thirteen times over the course of my career."

"They'd never see it coming," Dmitri offered, looking intrigued.

"He's right," Kevin said, still helpful. "I've never seen a receptionist anywhere near me those thirteen times."

"Shut up, Stone. You were useful for about eight seconds."

"Aw," Kevin said. "You sound mad."

The Boss cleared his throat. "It's quite a good idea, Jennifer, but Caitlyn's right—it's dangerous."

"Yes, but—if it'll help the Lieutenant get back into the Snakepit, it's worth it, don't you think? I mean, who knows what those bums are up to?"

"Who cares?" Caitlyn snapped, visibly upset.

"Caitlyn, they sent this guy to shoot your *best friend* in the face. Are you really going to stand for that?"

"No, but I'm not sending my *other* friend into the Snakepit, either. Think about what you're saying! We've got a building full of spies, but we've got to send *Jenny*? No offense, Jenn."

"This might be the twenty-first century," Jenny pointed out, "but still—when people see a petite, cute blonde, they blow her off. I've seen it since I was four. It's believable that I was a drone for The Boss, but not a field agent. They'll accept that Kevin could overpower me and bring me back for whatever *faux* info you'll give me."

"Bring *us* back," Caitlyn said promptly.

Kevin laughed. "Oh, honey. I'm good, but not that good. They'd never believe I could overpower a cyborg *and* a receptionist."

Jenny hid her grin behind her hand.

"Just me, then," Caitlyn suggested.

"No," The Boss said at once.

"It's not up to you," Caitlyn practically snarled.

"On that you are wrong, as you are so often, my dear."

"Why the hell *not*?"

"For the same reason Jenny's right. They'd never believe he could bring *you* back."

"They don't have to know—"

"You won't be able to resist tossing minions over railings. And the first blood test they do, they *will* know. Not to mention, as you tirelessly remind me, you don't work for me."

"Neither does Jenny!"

He ignored the outburst. "But a 'drone', as Jenny put it—"

"What, you don't have an agent who looks innocent and kidnappable?"

"Don't you see, Caitlyn?" Jenny interrupted. "That's why

it's foolproof. Because if something goes wrong, nobody's out anything. The Boss doesn't lose a field agent, intel doesn't fall in the wrong hands, and the lieutenant can get safely back in."

"I'd never let anything happen to her," Kevin said quietly, if a bit muffled around the spork he was chewing.

"That's sweet," Caitlyn snapped, "but unrealistic. Why are we even considering this? And how many of those things do you keep on you at any given time?"

"Because it's a viable option," The Boss said, ignoring the other part of her question.

"Dude—if you do this, I'll never speak to you again."

"Promises, promises, dear."

"And I won't do any more jobs for you, either. And neither will my husband."

"Stop it, Caitlyn," Jenny said sharply. "You're my boss, not my mother."

"Don't call me that," Caitlyn begged. "I'm not your boss."

"Exactly. This is my decision, not yours, and it was my idea, I might add, not anyone else's, and we're going to do it, and that's how it is."

Kevin sighed and leaned back, smirking at The Boss. "It's great to have a real man in charge."

# Chapter 13

An hour later, it was decided. Dmitri had more or less dragged his wife out—she still had plenty to say on the subject—and Kevin went off to prep for the mission. The Boss had asked Jenny to remain for a while, and he was looking at her thoughtfully now.

She broke the long silence with a barely polite, "What?"

"You know, Jennifer, you don't have to prove anything to anybody. You're a successful young woman. You're not defined by what you do."

"Hmmph," she replied with a skeptical twist of the mouth.

"If I could hazard a guess—were your parents drug addicts, or perhaps alcoholics?"

She smiled a bit and tilted her head.

"It's quite typical for the child of such parents to think his—or her—worth is measured by how useful they are. How helpful they can be to others. How many problems they can solve, in tough spots. How many—"

"So I don't like sitting on my hands," she interrupted as gently as she could, feeling the smile dry up on her face. "That proves, what exactly?"

"Not a thing. Off the topic entirely, how attached are you

to keeping your current managerial position at Caitlyn's salon?"

"Extremely," she lied.

Now it was his turn to give a skeptical look.

"Even if I wasn't, what use am I beyond this particular mission? I'm nobody special. I can't do things like Caitlyn and Dmitri. I'm just a, a nobody," she said again, because she couldn't think of a better descriptive term.

"Jennifer." The Boss shook his sleek head. "Remind me to throttle the gentleman—it always seems to be a man—who put such shitty ideas in your pretty head." He sighed when she betrayed no reaction, and changed the subject. "Do you understand exactly what it is you're supposed to do?"

"Accompany Kevin back to his Snakepit contacts and verify his account of attempts to complete their mission for him. Once they accept him, submit to what Kevin believes will be a mild interrogation process for a civilian captive. Observe the initial stages of Kevin's sabotage of the Snakepit, within a day or so. When the moment arrives and he releases me from captivity, run like hell."

"Comparisons are odious—"

"John Donne. And Cervantes."

"—but this is *such* a pleasant change from Caitlyn. Keep an eye on Lieutenant Stone," he added. He looked down at himself and seemed surprised to see the rose boutonnière, looking pretty bedraggled after the day it had had. Jenny wondered how the EMTs had worked around it, how he'd gotten his bulletproof vest off without disturbing it. A puzzle for another day.

"The man was playing a part for years," The Boss continued. "He might have forgotten about the real Kevin Stone."

"Yes," she said again; it was a thought that had occurred to her many times.

"Do you have any weapons experience?"

"Yes—I can hit the ten-spot about ninety-five percent of the time with my Beretta."

"Self-defense? Karate, judo, aikido?"

"I have a brown belt in judo, a black in aikido."

"Any special licensing, degrees?"

"I had a double major in Marketing and Criminal Psychology. I'm fifteen credits away from my master's in psychology."

"Anything else?"

"No."

"Are you sure?"

"Oh, right." She had forgotten. "I'm a licensed EMT in the state of Minnesota."

"And you're—"

"Twenty-three." She answered his unspoken question. "There's never anything good on TV."

He actually rubbed his hands together. "And you've been spending your entire life trying to make yourself useful, probably trying to get your father's attention—"

"Boss," she said, "your ability to take advantage of my fragile emotional state, born of years of verbal parental abuse, is . . . well, limited."

"Ha," he said dourly.

"This isn't about pleasing you. Or annoying Caitlyn. That's just, you know, a bonus. It's not even about protecting Stacy. For once, maybe this once, it's about me. It's like, well, a *non*-movie, you know?"

"No."

"If this was a sci-fi flick, Caitlyn would be the star. If it was an action movie, Dmitri would be the star. Romance— maybe you and Stacy together. Well, there is no movie for people like me. But I'm the star, anyway."

"Movie or not, it all ends when you catch a bullet between those pretty baby blues," The Boss added with grating cheer.

"Plenty more where I came from."

He rolled his eyes and stretched his neck, looking like a mildly pissed-off seal anxious for his morning fish bucket. "Jenny m'dear, if there were plenty more like you, I'd send another one in your place."

# Chapter 14

Jenny almost smiled; like any gun range, the place had the comforting smell of metal, gun oil, gunpowder, and burned paper.

"At least he didn't just drop you over the Snakepit on your word you can take of yourself," Caitlyn bitched from the shooter's bench behind her.

"It's something to pass the time," she replied calmly, popping the last round into the clip, then sliding the clip into the pistol. She sighted downrange, glanced to the left, saw all lights were green, and emptied the gun at the paper target.

"Ninety-eight," Caitlyn said.

"Are you sure?" A ninety-eight would mean she wasn't entirely in the black on two of the targets.

"Helloooooo? Super vision over here."

Jenny hit the button, which brought the targets on their slow, rumbling track toward her. As they got closer, she saw Caitlyn was right.

She scowled at the ruined paper. "I guess I was a little nervous."

"You still hit all the centers—just not entirely in the center. I mean, jeez, I didn't know you could do that. *When* do you do that? It must take—I dunno—years of practice."

"Years," she agreed.

"This whole place gives me the creeps," Caitlyn admitted in a low voice. "A shooting range in the basement, and The Boss on the top floor. And any number of horrors in between."

"I kind of like it," she said, popping the clip. She pulled out the earplugs and set them on the waist-high table beside her. This was a small lie; she'd never in her life been alone in a shooting range—except for Caitlyn, that is. Alone, no shooters to call the safety checks, no one to spot for her, no one to good-naturedly kid her about a date on Saturday night.

Just loud shots, echoing concrete, and Caitlyn's occasional commentary.

"So, you can shoot," she said glumly.

"Don't sound so surprised. I have a life," she teased, "outside of running your salon."

"Don't remind me. Apparently a secret life of bullets and karate. Cripes."

She opened a new box of bullets, loaded the clip again, slid the clip back into the gun, popped her plugs back in, said, "Clear, range," out of force of habit, and squeezed (never pulled) the trigger a few more times. It wasn't her gun, but it was a good one, all the same.

"One hundred—there, are you happy now?"

"Sure."

"Seeing as how we're alone and all—if I can get you to stop banging away with that thing for five seconds—"

"Don't bother, Caitlyn."

Her friend made a face and got up from the folding chair, looking like she wanted several wet naps. Jenny had to smile. Like all gun ranges, this one had a hint of grime about it. All the powder flying in the air at all hours, such places were impossible to keep clean. At least they'd changed out of their bridesmaid dresses.

"Don't bother, she tells me."

"Who are you talking to?" Jenny asked.

"You know how nuts this is, right?"

"Sure," Jenny replied. "That's why I want to go."

# Part Two

# WITHOUT*

*Defined by *Merriam-Webster* as: 1. outside; 2. the lack of
something or someone.

# Chapter 15

As she stretched out in the back of the navy blue Ford minivan, Jenny couldn't help feeling abnormally cheerful. And not just because of all the legroom, either.

Okay, she had a splitting headache. And a long drive (well, Kevin had a long drive), since she'd refused any sleep medication. Shoot, she wouldn't take a Tylenol for a stab wound—she was well aware that her risk of becoming an addict was much higher than the average bear's.

*And* she was going into unimaginable danger with a man she'd only met yesterday. A double agent no one quite trusted, no less. A gorgeous, buff redneck whose arms were as big around as her thighs, a man with eyes like chocolate and a smile like the sun breaking through the clouds. He smelled like gunpowder and soap. It made her crazy. She blamed the good smell. No, the eyes. No, the incredible body. No, her essential weakness, spotted early on by her father and nurtured by same.

No, the eyes.

So, she was in a fix. But unlike poor Caitlyn, she was in a mess of her own making. She should have gone back to her nice, safe job at Mag, or her nice, safe apartment in Maplewood. She *should* have run the minute she realized The

Boss had been shot. But no, here she was, bound (not yet literally, but soon) for the Snakepit.

Still. Being cheerful made sense for her, at least. Unlike Caitlyn, she *welcomed* these changes to her life. Twenty-four hours ago she had been dateless at the biggest wedding Minneapolis had ever seen.

Not to mention covered in frosting, with nary a man interested enough to make bold and suggestive comments. Dateless bridesmaids were their own pathetic species: at least you could usually hook up with a groomsman. But not her, The Bridesmaid Who Always Missed.

And not at *that* wedding—The Boss, curiously, had no groomsmen except for Dmitri, who was very married. There hadn't been time to flirt, much less trade phone numbers. Even the paramedics were too quick for her.

Lame, so lame.

At least she'd gotten out of doing the Electric Slide (she always tripped over the hem of her gown before the second verse; they *should* be singing, *She's a trippin' like a moron, she's a-stumblin' like an epileptic.* But never mind.).

Not to mention avoiding the tiresome jostling for the thrown bouquet. Stupid superstition: she'd caught three in the last five years.

In fact, the whole morning had been one reminder after another that she was doomed to die alone, in sweatpants, with half her face chewed off by her cats. Not that she had any. Well, she had lots of sweatpants, just no cats. But the road she was traveling, it was inevitable.

But no longer! That was why she'd insisted on tagging along with Kevin. She'd taken advantage of The Boss's unscrupulousness, ignored Caitlyn's howls of protests, and tried not to glance at Kevin too often out of the corner of her eye.

Now here she was, mistress of her own destiny . . . or, at least, mistress of the back of the minivan. Off to places unknown! The Snakepit! Wherever that was! Saving the world and all that good shit. Unless Kevin turned on her and shot her in the face. Not that she could imagine him doing such a thing. But she was new to the game. You never could tell. Still, it was better than cutting wedding cake at a reception.

*(You're not smart enough for this.)*

She ignored the thought, wondering just how long the car ride would be. As his "prisoner," she shouldn't talk to Kevin. She couldn't even see him, stretched out in the back like she was.

*(Go home, kid. You'll never pull it off.)*

It had been a long day, and a longer night. She was low on sleep—and boyfriends. So she closed her eyes and dozed.

# Chapter 16

She awoke an undefined amount of time later, completely disoriented. Why was it so dark? What was wrong with her arms?

"What the hell?"

She could hear the van slowing. "Sorry," Kevin called back. "We're getting close. I couldn't exactly pull up to the Snakepit, *then* put the cuffs on, right?"

"You blindfolded me and cuffed me in my *sleep?*"

He sounded wounded. "You were sleeping so sound, I couldn't stand to wake you up."

"I'm having flashbacks to Homecoming," she muttered, wriggling. Louder, she said, "That's pretty creepy, Kevin."

"I thought you'd be glad to get more sleep. I mean, it's not like you'll have tons of naptime surrounded by Snakepit guards."

She knew she was a sound sleeper, but this was ridiculous. She puffed a breath through the side of her mouth, but the blindfold didn't budge. And he was still talking, still sounding a little hurt. The bum.

"And if you're getting cold feet, hon, I think this is a real good time to speak up. There's plenty of time to turn back."

"I just have a mild objection to being handcuffed and

blindfolded in my sleep," she snapped. "Let's not make it like it's a big emotional problem I'm having, okay?"

"Okay, okay. Don't get your Irish up."

"How'd you know I was Irish?" she asked suspiciously.

"With that skin?"

"Never mind my skin."

"Women."

"What was that?"

"Uh, nothing."

"Don't make me come up there."

"You got no problem going in with me, being interrogated by various bad guys, possibly getting shot at—but you're pissed because I didn't wake you up when I put the agreed-upon cuffs on you?"

"I guess it's just the reality setting in. Like a head cold. I'll get over it."

"Maybe we should go back."

"Don't you dare."

"Well, good. 'Cuz we're here. It'll be just a quick walk."

"I'm ready to stretch my legs."

She heard him shut off the engine, heard the creak of the door opening and the *chunk!* as he slammed it closed. Heard the back door of the minivan wheeze open. He bent in and she said, "Kiss me for luck."

"You have to do it twice," he said, his breath tickling her nose, "for it to be really lucky." She felt his firm mouth on hers, had a vague thought (the Snakepit surveillance couldn't see into the van, right? It just looked like he was leaning in to pull her out, right?) that she couldn't quite bring to the top of her brain, kissed him back. His breath smelled like strawberry Mentos. The freshmaker!

He kissed her a second time, a quick peck on the side of her mouth, then muttered, "Last chance."

"Years too late," she replied.

# Chapter 17

"Stone, Kevin P., with prisoner in transit. Here to see Charmer."

Kevin was speaking into the small speaker on the wall, one hand pressed, fingers spread wide, on the wall pad. The other was gripping Jenny by her right elbow as her wrists flexed in the cuffs. Her arms were still weak from their encounter in the minivan, but she found enough strength to jerk away from him and spit. While she couldn't see through her blindfold, she was sure there were cameras watching, and they agreed she needed to put up a bit of a show.

He almost smiled at her performance, but resisted the impulse. This wasn't the most dangerous part of the mission, but it was definitely in the top three.

Was he focused? No, he was admiring the way she filled out her drab office skirt, her blouse, the way her blond hair had been piled into an efficient bun, a few honey-colored strands straggling into her face. She was probably nervous—*he* was nervous!—but she looked like a woman waiting for a bus.

Four hours of sleep in the minivan. He was yanking her into harm's way and she had snored. He couldn't blame The Boss for his recruiting proclivities—but part of him hated the man all the same. Jenny should be—he didn't know, knitting or something. Not cuffed and dressed like a clerk and waiting to be interrogated.

"Welcome back, Stone," a dulcet voice came from the speaker. "You're cleared for entry. And . . . you've brought me a present!"

"Yup."

"To make up for your abysmal fuck-up in Minneapolis."

"Yup."

"Mmmm." There was a silence, a click, and then the giant doors at the end of the corridors slowly slid open.

*Thank you, Jesus.* The Snakepit's chief had to be dying of curiosity. The face-to-face meetings would be perilous. He had to debrief the Snakepit leadership, keep Jenny out of trouble, gather as much intel as he could, prepare whatever blow he could muster to the organization, grab her from whatever dungeon they would stick her in, and get back to O.S.I. before the shit really hit the fan.

*What was I thinking? Why didn't I just come back alone and take my chances?*

He led Jenny to the doors, which were yawning before them like the mouth of a giant. He wanted to give her a word of comfort, but didn't dare. He also wanted to bury his nose under the hair by her ear and lick her throat; but that was probably also a bad idea.

Much too belatedly, he started to wonder what the hell he'd been thinking when he'd agreed to this crazy idea. Was it just to save his own ass? Was that really it? Was he that selfish?

Or did he just admire her bravery, and want to see what

she did next? His knees were almost buckling, but whether it was shame, admiration, or nerves, he had no idea.

The Snakepit was run by Charmer, a brittle-looking brunette in her early thirties with a porcelain complexion and a narrow mouth. Her staff found her code name ironic for several reasons, but mostly because she was not in the least charming. She was dressed like an undertaker having a good year: cashmere, black, tailored.

Also, she'd seen one too many Kill Bill movies; all her people had reptile code names. It was pretty silly, when you got right down to it. Let the flyboys have their call signs, let the grunts just get the job done. But who was going to argue with her?

"Welcome back, Sidewinder."

He restrained himself from an eye-roll. "Thanks, Charmer."

"Do you want to explain," Charmer continued, her right hand slipping out of sight, "why I'm not shooting you right now?"

"Curiosity killed the cat?" he guessed.

Her right hand stayed out of sight and she didn't reply. Kevin got down to business. "Brought a member of the new Wagner Team from O.S.I. Her name's Jennifer Branch. That's all I've gotten out of her so far."

"Oh, Sidewinder. How hard did you try?"

He shrugged with a grin. "I figured you'd want to do most of the work here. Thought you might pick her brain, find some good stuff."

"And let you back in my good graces."

"Yup."

"For missing the bride."

"Sorry. The Boss moved to adjust her veil, I think, and got right in my sights at the wrong time."

"At least he's not dead," Charmer said. "That would be awful." She spoke with total sincerity, then reached up to Jenny's face and pulled the blindfold down. "And you, Ms. Branch. What's your story?"

Jenny blinked and looked around. The bad guy's lair looked uncomfortably like any other office she'd ever been in. Sideboard, moat-like desk, cheap carpeting, drawn cream-colored blinds, memos stuck to a corkboard behind and above Charmer's head.

"My story? Why give it now, when he tells me you're going to torture me for it later anyway?"

"Sidewinder's been filling your head with silly ideas," Charmer sniped, and then licked her thin, colorless lips as she stared at Jenny's chest. "I don't torture civilians, unless they ask nicely."

"Oh. Well, I'm sure that won't be necessary."

Charmer's lips twitched, which Kevin assumed was some sort of tic, as he'd never seen her smile.

"So. Wagner Team. That could be useful. I'm tired of running the nanobyte race with those fascists, and losing."

*Oh, they're the fascists?* "I don't know why your man thought I would be valuable," Jenny volunteered with just the right desperation in her voice. "They don't let me see much around there. I'm just in admin, I'm not a scientist."

Now Charmer *did* smile, showing distinctly British teeth. Her Northern European accent was hard to place, though: part upper-class clipped English, with the slurs and burrs of Irish and Scots. A well-traveled woman.

"Ah," she was saying. "Secretaries know . . . *everything*. I'll take a clerk over a management head any day . . . or one of these reptiles that work for me."

"Thanks, Charmer," Kevin said dryly.

Charmer wrapped a wiry hand over Jenny's left shoulder.

Kevin watched Jenny shift her weight—he knew how uncomfortable being cuffed behind the back could get.

"I hope," the brunette whispered into Jenny's ear, "that you didn't sign any nondisclosure agreements with your employer."

Jenny cleared her throat and looked down at her feet. Kevin wondered how much of this nervousness was really an act. "Um, none that I won't break happily if you show me a dentist's drill."

"*Really?*" Charmer laughed, delighted. "Oh, dear, it will be a shame to let you go, after we've pumped you for information. You're so . . . accommodating."

Jenny looked up, a glint in her eye. "And you . . . keep pausing . . . like this."

Charmer dropped her hand and gave her an ugly look. "Sidewinder, take her down to the third floor . . . Dr. Loman will be waiting for you. Tell him to make her . . . comfortable, at least until I arrive." She seemed to hear the unnatural pauses in her voice, and tried to stop. She finished rapidly. "Then come back here. *Right* back. I want to hear all about the last day."

"Yes, ma'am." He jerked Jenny toward the door. "Let's go."

"Thanks for dropping by, Ms. Branch!" Charmer called after them in a high, childish voice. "I'll see you again once you're settled! Bye-bye!"

Jenny stumbled, and he couldn't blame her. Because Charmer had sounded perfectly warm and accommodating; it was possible she thought she meant it. It was creepier than the woman's out-and-out meanness.

*Great*, Kevin chastised himself. *As if I didn't know it before, I sure as shit know it now: Charmer was either born insane, or it was a long, slow process. Either way, Jenny could be in some trouble. Is it worse that she's nuts, or better?*

He steadied her, his fingers closing over her arm in what he hoped was an impersonal, stormtrooper-type embrace. And tried not to think of the next few hours, which were bound to be right tricky.

For both of them.

# Chapter 18

"**D**r. Loman?" Jenny asked, being met quite courteously by a fellow who didn't look much older than she was. "As in Willy?"

"Not hardly, chickie." So much for courtesy. He snorted and jerked his head, flipping a hank of dirty blond hair out of his face. He was wearing a white lab coat over a tee-shirt that read FREE KATIE AND DIE, whatever that meant. His jeans were faded, almost white at the knees, and his sneakers were so dirty it was impossible to tell what color they had been originally.

He was about Caitlyn's height (which meant he towered over her) but much leaner, almost bony. His horn-rimmed glasses hid dust-colored, darting eyes. In five seconds he'd looked at her boobs, her face, her neck, her boobs, her stomach, her boobs, and her eyes.

"Sorry about keeping the cuffs on," he said without a trace of regret in his voice. "Procedure."

"Uh-huh." She looked around the small, clean sitting room. For the root of all evil, so far the Snakepit hadn't been so bad. She wondered what Kevin was doing upstairs with Charmer.

*(You're not s'posed to be here, but you are, so you might as well pay attention.)*

"Is this where you whip out the hot pokers?"

He took her by the elbow and practically dragged her into the lab. Funny. When Kevin touched her like that she hadn't minded, had even welcomed his strong fingers on her arm. When Dr. Loman did it, it was quite the opposite. It was like being touched by mean worms.

"Hell, no!" he was chortling. "What year do you think this is? Nobody does that stuff anymore, not with all the good drugs we've got."

"I'm allergic to several barbiturates," she informed him.

"I guess we'll just have to experiment then, won't we?"

"What a fine use of your Hippocratic oath," she commented, and he jerked her forward so hard she stumbled onto the exam table. With rough hands he flipped her over and spread her ankles out to strap them to the table. She tried not to squirm; lying on her hands was incredibly uncomfortable.

"You know dick about me," he retorted. "I've got bills to pay and a family to support."

"You and Dr. Mengele."

"Oh, like the O.S.I. is a bunch of choir angels?"

"We don't go around shooting brides, we don't kidnap people, and we don't—" She trailed off, because really, she had no idea *what* they did. Only that Caitlyn and Dmitri would never do the occasional "errand" for The Boss unless he was fundamentally good.

"The O.S.I. is a bunch of federally funded thinkers and drinkers. At least we stand on our own two feet."

"Yeah, right on top of other people's necks."

His mouth tightened down so far his lips actually disappeared. "Just shut up."

" 'Just shut up'? That's your big comeback?"

"I get the whole 'brave little detainee' thing, but it's wasted on me."

"Like mouthwash?" she suggested brightly.

He scowled. "I prefer to use drugs, but I *could* find a hot poker with a little effort." He readied a needle, twisted her onto her side by her arm, and plunged the sharp into the crook of her elbow with no warning.

"You didn't even swab me with alcohol," she protested.

"Least of your problems," he grunted, straightening.

"This is awkward," she said after a long silence. "What should we talk about?"

"That's also gonna be the least of your problems, sweetie."

"Did you know," she informed him, looking up, "that the ceiling is drifting down? I mean, you're kind of an ass and you deserve to have the ceiling squish you, but you should save yourself while you still can."

He ignored the ceiling, which somehow managed to keep descending without squishing anybody, and hooked her up to a few machines, letting his fingers linger as he trailed electrodes over her body. Then he was looking at her pupils with an annoying little light and listening to her heart.

Out of pure piss-headedness, he squeezed the blood pressure cuff a few times too many, and her arm went the color of a toad's stomach. Reaching casually toward a shelf, he flipped the red switch on an audio recording device. "Tell me about your work with the Wagner group."

"Now? How do you even know the stuff is working? You *just* gave it to me."

He seized her nipple through her thin shirt and twisted. "You probably can't feel that anymore. In fact, I doubt if you'd feel it if I removed the nipple entirely."

"You probably don't get a lot of second dates, do you?"

"Just answer, blondie."

"What was the question again?"

He reminded her, as he readied a shallow tray of metallic implements she couldn't quite see.

She told him everything.

# Chapter 19

She remembered little of what she said—all the stuff the O.S.I. techs had planted in her brain the night before, she supposed. Gobs and gobs of disinformation, sprinkled with a few nuggets of real facts that wouldn't hurt anyone if they got out.

It took hours.

She thought.

The drugs made it hard to tell.

"Wakey wakey!" Dr. Loman was yelling in her ear. She jerked away from the sound and nearly fell off the couch.

"What?" Her voice sounded equal parts sleepy and annoyed.

"You sang like the proverbial canary, sugar bumps, just like I knew you would." He reached out and flipped the recording device off. His glasses slipped down his long nose and he batted them back up into the proper place with a careless swipe of his hand. "They didn't hire me for my looks, you know."

"I gathered. Can I have a glass of water?"

"No." He tweaked her nipple again, and this time it hurt. But she was relieved to see absolutely no scars or marks on her. Whatever the tray had held before, it was nowhere to be found now. "Charmer wants to see you."

"Great. Where's—" *Kevin,* she almost asked, then caught herself. She was a hostage; why should she give a rat's ass where her supposed captor was? "Where's the bathroom?"

"Gonna have to wait." He pinched her thigh, then moved in closer until he was pinching between her thighs. "You look so adorable, all muzzy and groggy and helpless. I've got a boner the size of Texas—can you tell?"

She wriggled. Yes, the nano-infected handcuffs had done their job nicely while she was out. Meanwhile, Dr. Disgusting had his hands on her breasts, was rubbing her stomach and watching her face with the greedy gaze of a starved crow. It wasn't anything about her specifically that gave him the thrill, she knew. She was just a worthless bitch to him.

*(To everyone, daughter.)*

What was turning him on was the thought that she was helpless. That he could do whatever he wanted.

And he began to do just that.

"Where *are* they?" Charmer asked petulantly. She bashed her rook against Kevin's pawn, sending it flying. "I sent for her five minutes ago. Your game is horrible today, Sidewinder."

"It's your own fault," he managed through gritted teeth. "You left her with the company perv."

"Yes, but he came so highly recommended," she said reproachfully. Her pout deepened. "I *want* to *see* her."

"I'll go." He stood. Just the thought of delicate Jenny in the hands of that maniac for the last three hours—it was enough to make him want to put a fist through the wall. It felt like he'd been crawling the walls for a week. He'd lost count of the number of times he'd checked his watch. "I'll go right now."

"You might as well." Charmer tossed the board to the carpet. "It's no fun when you're not paying attention."

"Yeah, well, sorry about that."

"You bloody well aren't!" she hollered after him, but he was jogging to the elevators and barely heard her.

# Chapter 20

"God," Dr. Loman was saying, hands busy, hands crawling, "I bet you taste like a peach."

The fluorescent lights were bouncing off his glasses; she couldn't see his eyes. It made her feel like a bug under a magnifying glass.

"I bet what I taste like is none of your business, you pathetic asshole." Why wasn't she scared? She *should* be scared. But then, she knew a few tricks this lab-coated moron couldn't dream of.

*You don't look like what you are*, Stacy had once told her. *I guess that's both good and bad. Depending.*

Yes, depending. And what was this? Was he—he was! Dr. Loman was climbing up on the exam table with a practiced smoothness that showed he'd done this before. That, more than anything else, made her shudder.

How many helpless detainees? How often before, during, and after a drugged interrogation? How far did he go? Did Charmer know? Did she care?

*Of course she doesn't care, none of them care—you're in bad-guy central, GET IT THROUGH YOUR HEAD!*

He was directly over her and she was repulsed to see the shine of drool on his chin—ugh, he was drooling over her like a rib roast, like a butcher's special. One spidery hand was busy worming up her shirt, the other busy on the bulge between his legs.

"I really like you," he said, and slurped the drool back into his mouth.

*Is that why you stupidly undid the ankle cuffs?*

"You're really cute," he added.

"Aw," she said, and kneed him in the groin. The blow had less than the desired effect, blocked by his own hand as it was, but she followed up by smacking her cupped hands over his ears.

He lost all interest in her, as well as his hard-on.

Clutching his head and screaming the thin, high scream of a cornered rabbit, he rolled off the table and onto the floor, hitting face first with a loud thud that should have been sickening, but which she liked just fine.

She sat up and shook her hands in front of her, ignoring the ache in her shoulders while watching the mottled, shredded metal fly off in all directions. Those metal-eating nanobytes were welcome to find whatever else in this room they cared to eat.

Where did the O.S.I. *get* this stuff?

And if Caitlyn was infected with them, if that was why she was such a speedy, strong freak, why-oh-why did she never complain? Jenny would have loved to be different. She was flat wallpaper, she blended, she looked like nobody and she *was* nobody, but it would be pretty neat to—

Her musings were interrupted when the door flew open, framing a wrathful Kevin Stone.

"Time to go already?" she asked brightly, hopping down and giving Dr. Loman a brisk kick in the jaw.

"I'm here," he said gravely, "to save you."

He marched over and gave Dr. Loman another kick, actually flipping the other man over on his back. Now Loman was in a fix: he wanted to cup his ears and cradle his ribs, and was about two limbs short.

"Perv," Kevin said. Another kick—*fump*. "Sicko." *Fump*. "Fuckhead." *Fump*. Loman was halfway across the exam room by now, semiconscious. "Asshat. Jerkoff. You don't. Treat. Girls. Like. That." Each word, spoken in a scary monotone, was punctuated by another *fump*. "We've talked. About this. Before."

"Stop, what are you doing?" she hissed, looking around for a surveillance camera. She could see one, but it was dark . . . no red light, no nothing. Did he turn it off post-interrogation? Or was it always off?

"I said. Saving you."

She grabbed an arm—it was like grabbing the trunk of a young tree—and yanked. It had all the effect of grabbing a young tree, too. "You're nuts! I'm your prisoner, remember? You kidnapped me and brought me to—uh—wherever we are—"

"Iowa."

"Right." She tugged harder. Enough with the kicking! "Iowa." Then she paused. "The Snakepit's in Iowa?"

"Did he hurt you, Jenny? Did he violate you?"

She could see the old kicking machine was getting ready to rev back up. "Of course not. He's a professional." A professional shitheap. "And in case you haven't noticed, I had things under control. Then you had to come bursting in here like Rambo on steroids—"

"What'd you do to him?" Kevin asked, squatting down to look at the now-unconscious Dr. Loman.

"I ruptured his eardrums. And possibly gave him a brain concussion. You know how it is: just a plain old good-bye would have been awkward."

He laughed in spite of himself, and she was absurdly pleased that she had lightened his puzzling, dark mood.

"Now will you get out of here? What if someone sees you in here? What if Charmer's watching?"

"What if he'd raped you?" Kevin asked, dangerously quiet. "What if he'd given you stitches where a lady never wants them? It's happened before. I kicked the shit out of him not six months ago."

"Again: how have you stayed undercover so long?"

He ignored her. "This was a shitty idea. I never should have agreed. I sold your body for my ticket of readmission."

She was amazed at the mood change. He hadn't been this pissed when he'd been in O.S.I. custody. She didn't think he could get pissed at all. "Will you take a pill? I'm sure we can find his stash. Just calm down. You are totally forgetting the plan."

"The plan fucking sucks."

"You're swearing in mixed company," she teased.

He remained a stone. "Let's get out of here."

"Back up, l'il buckaroo. Not without what we came for. Otherwise this has all been for nothing."

He took a steadying breath. "Charmer sent me to hurry you along. We didn't know what was keeping you, and she's impatient."

"That's interesting, a bad quality in the head of a splinter cell of psychos. No offense."

"None taken."

"Wow, you can talk without moving your teeth!"

Finally, he smiled again. "We'd better go, 'cuz I'm giving serious thought to breakin' all that boy's fingers."

"Yeah, well, I was getting there. Figured I'd try to find Charmer's office and tell her how I had to fend off her pet rapist. I can do helpless yet pissed," she added.

"Rapist?" he asked sharply.

"Never mind. I was coming, I just got a little, uh, side-tracked. Now will you please stop talking like you have any interest in my well-being? Remember? Me prisoner, you bad guy?"

"He unhooks the cameras," Kevin said with scary calm. "Audio only, for an accurate transcript of what the patient says . . . but not what she experiences. Everybody knows. Charmer tolerates it because he gets results. Nobody can hear or see us right now." He looked longingly at the bloody heap that was Dr. Loman. "It would be sooo easy. Just twist and snap."

She shuddered. "Never mind. You'd better bring me back to her office. Remember the plan."

"I been a soldier since you were in pigtails," he snapped in a thick southern accent. *Ah been.* "I don't need no reminders."

"No, but you do need English 101. That *is* English you're speaking, right?"

He didn't smile, just took a careful step toward her. "Are you hurt?" he asked quietly. "Did he hurt you?"

"In case you didn't notice—and I see you didn't—he didn't have a chance against me," she said. "I'm a U of M graduate. Fear the Golden Gophers!"

"I was, uh, real worried about you."

"I was worried about *you*, when you charged in here. How did you stay undercover for so long? How did you make it through the first year?"

"Prob'ly because I didn't have you to worry about." He put large fingers under her jaw and lifted her face to his. Then he kissed her as if he had all the time in the world, as if they were in someone's living room instead of the sickly beating heart of an Iowan splinter cell. He kissed her the way she'd longed to be kissed: with rough care and with gentle urgency.

*(Crazy crazy crazy.)*

She pulled back. It was much, much harder than screwing up her courage to climb into the back of the minivan. "We'd better get going."

"Uh-huh," he replied, hugging her.

"I meant to Charmer's office."

"Right." Now he was holding her at arm's length and looking at her thoughtfully. "You're a little 'un. If we did that much longer, I'd get a crick in my neck."

"So buy me a stool for my birthday. Come on, we're probably late for our debriefing with the psycho Iowan."

"*She's* not from Iowa. She just works there."

"When we step out of here, I'm your prisoner again."

"You kidding? After seeing what you did to Loman, I'm not going near you without at least six guns."

"You'd be amazed how often I've heard that after a first date."

"Never mind your dates." He looked around the room. "Where's the cuffs?"

"Gone with the wind." She pointed to a small pile of metal shavings at the foot of the table. "The nanos chomped through them while I was singing for Loman."

"They didn't hurt your wrists?" He took her hands and looked at them, then released her, seeming slightly embarrassed. "Guess not."

"Besides, you don't need cuffs on little old me. I've already given up all my intel. I'm a dead battery, a burned-out light bulb, pick your metaphor. Why, d'you think you need to put another set on me?"

He actually had a set hanging from his gun belt, which was annoyingly sexy. And she was *not* that kind of girl. Strictly vanilla for her . . .

But instead of making like Hutch, he said, "You're half my size, sweetie, and you're supposedly drugged to the gills. I think they'll understand if I don't truss you like a Christmas goose. How's the tooth?"

She probed her tongue into her back tooth, the wisdom tooth that had never needed to be pulled. There was a little flap of skin that hung just to the side of the thing, and the O.S.I. techs had stuffed it full of uppers. Sweet, sweet uppers.

Yes, she was supposed to be drugged to the gills, but the drugs had been doing their job nicely for the last five minutes, and she felt ready to take on the world. Snakepit. Whatever.

Maybe it was just the kiss.

"For the record, if you were a betting man, I'd tell you to bet that now's when Charmer tries to talk me into switching sides."

"Unless she decides to shoot you instead, since you're no more use."

"Nonsense! In case you haven't noticed, I'm irresistible to everyone in the Pit, not to mention O.S.I. Funny, my guidance counselor never hinted about any of this."

At last, he smiled. "Irresistible."

"Irresistible!"

"Yup. Just the word on my mind."

"Your tiny, overtaxed mind," she said cheerfully, and followed him out of the bleak lab.

# Chapter 21

*How did you stay undercover for so long? How did you make it through the first year?*

He gritted his teeth as he took Jenny gently (but convincingly) by the back of the neck and guided her down the hallway in front of him. It hadn't been a matter of making it, of course. It had been a matter of getting away. Distancing himself from the Stones. The joke that was the Stone crime syndicate.

*Twenty years ago*

He had to pee but if he got out of bed the clawset monster would get him. It was stupid and worse—it was baby stuff, pure Pampers crap, but it was also very, very dark. And the worker bees were upsetting his mother. The worker bees almost never came to the house, almost never late at night, and he wanted Daddy; Daddy would fix the worker bees and maybe come and check on him and Tom and Benny.

His mother's voice, raised in anger. Too many closed doors between him and her to make out what she was saying, but it sounded loud and angry and scared. What did she have to be scared of? Daddy took care of her, took care of all of them. And grown-ups didn't see clawset monsters. They didn't see anything, he sometimes thought.

He could hear stomping footsteps in the hall and shrank into himself, imagined himself a soccer ball, a baseball, a tennis ball, a Ping-Pong ball. Something wee and small, something easily overlooked.

In the bunk beds by the window, Tom and Benny slept on. The twins weren't afraid of anything. It was why he never talked about the clawset monster . . . his own little brothers weren't afraid of that baby stuff, and he was practically a grown-up man.

A real man would get out of the bed, cross the floor (evading the fabulous litter of toys the twins managed to leave, like snails with trails), open the bathroom door (ignoring the ajar closet door four feet to the left), go in, turn on the light, flip up the toilet lid, and pee.

A real man wouldn't be curled up like a shrimp, cupping his throbbing belly and wishing he had a transporter beam that would take him right to the—

His bedroom door was thrown open, spilling harsh light into the room. Kevin barely—just—avoided wetting his pajamas. The twins didn't even stir.

"You'll wake them," his mother said in a scoldy, scared voice. "Leave them be! My husband is coming! My husband is coming and he'll—he'll fix everything!"

"Mr. Stone's dead, ma'am. You and your children will be, too, if you don't come with me right now."

His mother swatted at the big man—Sean Garrit, Kevin saw, his daddy's number one helper—but to no effect. Mr. Garrit crossed the room and started shaking Ben awake.

"Kevin, get up, kid. We gotta go. Help your mom with your brothers."

"But I have to—"

"Now, kid."

Kevin got up. To his surprise, his mother was now meekly helping Mr. Garrit—Mr. Garrit, who wouldn't say shit if he had a mouthful. Mr. Garrit, who always joked about getting Daddy's job. In the gloom of the bedroom, he looked huge, though Kevin knew his daddy was much bigger.

"Is there—can I pack a couple of—"

"No time, Mrs. Stone. We gotta get in the wind yesterday. You can buy clothes and stuff once we're clear of Chicago."

"But my family—the others—"

"Don't you get it, Mrs. Stone? *You're* the only ones left. Now come on!"

"But all the—the others—"

"Worm food, courtesy of the FBI. You want your boys in lockdown before the sun comes up? Those feds got itchy trigger fingers, Missus, and you wouldn't be the first syndicate wife to hit the bricks tonight."

Kevin squatted and groped around the carpet while his mom and Mr. Garrit were pulling the sleepy twins from their bunks. His fingers passed over several chewed sporks (his daddy loved original-recipe KFC and they went to the Colonel's every Saturday), and closed over the lava rock Daddy brought back from his last trip. It fit in his hands like a small brick.

"Let's go, Stones. Right now."

Stumbling and still more asleep than awake, the twins followed their mother, who was following Mr. Garrit. Mr. Garrit, the man Daddy said could squat and lean and had maybe a few too many thoughts about moving up when he should be happy to stay put. Mr. Garrit, the only one who had come to the house tonight. The brains, his daddy called him. "I'm the boss, but he's the brains." Then his daddy would laugh and laugh.

Could it be true? Was Daddy dead? It seemed impossible, too huge for his tired child's mind to grasp; he might as well imagine God being dead.

But it made no sense—why would the FBI kill his daddy? His daddy was a good guy—he protected businesses; that was his job. The FBI (as his daddy had told him on more than one occasion) should give him a medal.

And where were the other guys? Mr. Brady, Mr. Shea, Mr. Flanagan, Mr. Barron, Mr. Donovan? If there was a *(shootout, like in the Westerns)* problem, Mr. Garrit would be the first one to get shot, the last one to run off and help the boss's family. Because he seemed nice, and sometimes he talked nice, and sometimes he brought them nice things, but inside, way down deep, he was *(crazy crazy crazy)* a man who didn't really care about them. Kevin's daddy didn't notice, or didn't care; either way, it was none of his business and all of Daddy's.

Kevin took a moment to dart into the bathroom and take a leak. He found he couldn't; any desire to pee had been swallowed up by the awful fear that *(Daddy's dead)* things had gone very, very badly.

He adjusted his PJ bottoms and hurried toward the living room, taking just enough time to lift the lava rock from the counter on his way out the bathroom door. He could hear voices now, as he got closer; his mama had been right—this house was too big for five people.

But he had the feeling new people would be living in the Stone mansion very soon, so what did it matter that it was too big, had always been too big?

Mama: "What are you doing? Do you hear something?"

Mr. Garrit: "You know, I always liked you, but I kinda hated you, too. You always acted like you were too good for me."

Mama: "Put that away and help me with these children. This is no time for one of your stupid jokes."

"Joke's on you, Missus Stone. Or, Widow Stone, I guess. The FBI didn't kill your man—they'd much rather have seen him on trial. But who do you think would go to jail if Jack Stone cut a deal? I buried his garbage for ten . . . damn . . . years. And I'm telling you right now, after tonight, I'm through with Stone shit."

Kevin hurried around the corner, his arm cocked, the lava rock firm in his fist, and he was getting ready to bean Mr. Garrit a good one when the front door crashed open and his daddy staggered into the room.

"Cripes on a cracker! My arm feels like it's on *fire*."

"Goddammit," Mr. Garrit fumed, "how many times do I have to shoot at you?"

"Not no more," his daddy said, and Kevin thought, *bang*, but Mr. Garrit shouldn't have turned his back on Mama, because she was on him like a wildcat and rode Mr. Garrit all the way down, cracking his head on the coffee table for good measure.

"You believe this shirt?" his daddy was grumping. Blood was streaming down the shoulder, ruining the flawless white. "Brand new and now I gotta toss it."

"Shame on you! This makes, what? Third time this year? How many times I gotta say it? Stop telling your underlings enough info to let them take over the organization."

"Aw, Daddy," Kevin said, coming down the stairs. "You blabbed at work again?"

"Awwww," his daddy whined, "we was just shooting the breeze. It gets so boring at work—it's hard to think of new things to talk about."

His mama was rubbing her forehead like she did when she got one of her sick headaches. "For God's sake, Tom."

"Besides, who'd want my job? I been shot at more than a Thanksgiving Tom."

The twins were yawning and standing over Mr. Garitt's unconscious body. Benny opened his eyes wide and said, "I guess we're gonna move again."

"You guessed right," Mama said.

# Chapter 22

*Nine years ago*

Kevin sat down across from his little brother. They had been given a private room, ostensibly not bugged, but of course they both knew better. Not that Benny would think twice about shooting his mouth off.

"So, you gonna do it?" he said by way of greeting.

"Benny. Not only did you knock over all those ATMs with a butter knife, but you got caught on camera each time."

His brother scowled, looking like a younger, jowlier version of Richard Nixon. "I never looked straight at the camera."

"Not to mention, you've got the millions that dad gave us when you came of age, so there's absolutely no reason to rob anybody. At all. And yet, that's what you do. It's what you always do."

"Yeah, it's hard to get your hands on some cash on a Friday night."

"You could just use your ATM card on a Friday night."

"Well. Uh."

Kevin rubbed his temples. "What."

"All my money's tied up in oil wells in New York."

"There are no oil wells in New York."

"Not yet," his brother said, winking slyly.

*God, God, help me not to strangle him . . . give me strength . . .*
"You pissed away all your money on a scam," he said. It
wasn't a question.

"Look, if you just testify that we were together that
night—"

And the night of the nineteenth. And the twenty-second.
And the thirtieth. And the third. And the ninth. And the
eleventh. And—"

"So, you gonna?"

"Benny, listen carefully. I told Daddy and I told Mama
and I told both of you boys and now I'm telling you again:
I'm out. I'm not helping you. I'm one of the good guys. Get
it?"

His brother looked vague. "No."

"I. Am. A. Good. Guy. I. Can't. Help. You."

"Yeah, but that's part of your secret plan, right?"

"My secret plan to go straight."

"So." His brother seemed to be having trouble following.
Which meant it was a day of the week that ended with a Y.
The twins were admirably following in the Stone family
footsteps. "You're not gonna testify?"

"Little brother, I'm gonna be in the wind about five minutes after I leave this rathole."

His brother brightened. "Then maybe Tommy can—"

"He's prepping his own trial."

"Yeah, well. Our lawyers say—"

Kevin got up. "I don't want to hear it." He knocked on
the locked door and once again squashed the urge to choke
his brother. "A butter knife, for God's sake?"

Benny shuddered. "After the way we grew up? I fuckin'
hate guns. Don't tell Mama I swore."

"Don't worry," he said, and left when the guard opened the door.

*Six years ago*

"Congratulations, Mr. Stone. Only one person in ten thousand gets this far."

"Thank you, Director."

"Are you sure you don't want the slot in Behavioral Sciences? You've got the background for it."

"No thank you, Director."

"Strictly undercover, then."

"Yes."

"Well, we won't keep you here. We're farming you out to a small FBI-funded cell, Covert Ops Protection—"

"The C.O.P.s, yes, Director."

"I hate acronyms," Director MacCabe muttered, producing a scowl that made her look almost unattractive. Her hair was more gray than red, but she had the freckles and green eyes straight from County Butler. "That's all it is around here: C.O.P., O.S.I., F.B.I., C.I.A., S.S.C., A.T.F.—gives me a migraine just thinking about it."

"Perhaps an IV of drugs ASAP on the QT, ma'am."

"Hilarious, Stone." She closed his file and pushed it away. "Your psych eval came back just fine, by the way."

"Thank you, Director."

"Remarkable, considering what you went through as a child. And as a teenager. And last year. Quite, uh, quite a family tree, Stone."

"It's okay, Director. You can say it. I come from a long line of criminally deranged morons."

"I didn't, uh, say that. Exactly."

Kevin yawned.

"Am I *boring* you, Stone?"

"Yes, ma'am."

"Well, too bad. This was, I'm sure you recall, your second psych eval."

"Yes."

"Because the first headshrinker thinks the pressure of undercover work will crack you like an egg under a sneaker, bring back childhood trauma, send you over to the dark side as you're supposedly genetically inclined, blah-blah."

"Kind of you to arrange another test, ma'am, as opposed to, say, what might be best for me."

"Yes, very kind. The first doc had a known prejudice against the new C.O.P. program. Not to mention organized crime. So we found another one, and she thinks you'll do well."

"Ma'am, I—" *know all this already*, he tried to say.

"This is the part where you tell me you were born for this job." Her smile took the sting out of the words.

"No, ma'am, I wasn't born for it. I was made for it when I was just a kid down South."

"Yes, a budding member of the Stone crime syndicate . . . you would have been the third generation."

"Would have. Maybe." Even now, it haunted him: was he in the law as a matter of rebellion, or because he was so disgusted by the general idiocy of his family? They were ruthless, they were rich, they were idiots. His father was the Southern Clouseau: he had missed more assassination attempts by virtue of tripping or forgetting a meeting or getting drunk at the wrong time than he ever did by simple avoidance. So the question remained—would he have followed in his father's footsteps if he had been more like them? Or had the urge to be the black sheep of the syndicate shoved him toward the FBI, to this stinking little office in this teeming, furious town, surrounded by crooked Yankees and too many guns?

"It doesn't bother you? Talking about them?"

"No. I don't see them anymore, anyway." Had fled from them, in fact. Was going undercover to avoid being asked, yet again, to perjure himself in court. No, my father didn't break that guy's arm and then fall into the river. No, my brother didn't steal a tray of cream puffs and get pulled over because his taillight was out. No, my mother didn't shoot the butcher over a poorly cut pork loin. "It's finished business."

"Sing it again, Stone," the director said, and that was that, meeting over.

# Chapter 23

*Four years ago*

"It's called the Snakepit."

"Yes, and it's mine, right?" Kevin had to actively restrain himself from leaping over the desk and choking the intel out of the boss C.O.P. "The assignment? I'm going? It's mine, right?"

"Simmer down, l'il camper. You've been here—what? Two y—"

"Two years, two months, eighteen days."

"Are you all right? You look like you're gonna stroke out."

"I've waited a long time for this."

"Well, you're freaking me out. Take a breath. Lean back." The boss C.O.P. laughed. "You look like you're going to come over the desk at me."

"Too many Diet Cokes today, sir."

"That stuff's poison," the boss C.O.P. said absentmindedly, still poring over the paperwork spread all over his desk. He had the stooped shoulders and thin smile of a desk sergeant. His hair was carefully combed from ear to ear. His suit was strictly off the rack. He had a smiley face tattooed over the third knuckle of his left hand. "You should drink at least eight bottles of water a day."

"Or I could just slit my wrists," he suggested.

The boss C.O.P. looked up. "Stone, are you sure you want this?"

"I have a choice?" he asked with mock amazement.

"Sure. This will take months out of your life. You'll probably end up with a bullet in your brain for your pains. The woman who runs the Pit is too young for the job, and stone crazy to boot."

"But I'll get to go in, right? I can start? They'll think I'm a double agent?"

"You are," he reminded him, "just for us, not them. Stone, why the almighty rush? You could have had your pick, you ended up with the Feebs. They punted you to us. Now you're chomping to go to the Snakepit. Is this about your family?"

"Of course it is."

"Because the last trial is just about over, and you weren't going to testify, anyway—"

"There will be another trial. And another. And one after that. They're too dumb to quit. And they'll never have enough."

The man had the grace to pause. "Right. Dumb question, but I had to ask. You're sort of famous, you know— Mob kid gone good."

He ignored the Boss C.O.P.'s awkward kindness. "If I can get in there, I'll kick that place apart like it was a pile of sand. No more bank shakedowns, no more intel stealing, no more innocent people killed because they found out the wrong thing at the wrong time. I want those fuckers in the ground six months after I walk in the front door."

"Eeeeeasy, Stone. You're frothing." He flipped through more paperwork. "And apparently you're not crazy. No more than the rest of us, anyway."

"Don't worry. I'll get the job done. What about my handler?"

"Not this time—too dangerous. If you need extraction, call the S.A.T. line. Otherwise, no talking to the good guys. Remember, you're a jaded, annoyed, pseudo-good guy who hates the low pay and the long hours. Why would you ever talk to one of your old co-workers? You're a Stone—bad guys pepper your family tree. It's only natural you'd want to switch sides."

"Yes," he murmured, "only natural."

"A handler leaves you too exposed."

*And slows me down*, he thought but didn't say.

"You only contact us to warn us, or to get out. But essentially, this will be a fact-gathering mission. Probably only take six months, at least to start."

"ID?"

"All righteous. You're going in as yourself, a Stone from C.O.P. Another double agent in place is going to pave the way for you, 'recruit you' to the Pit just before he pulls out. Let 'em run your papers—you'll come up clean. You'll be who you say you are. That should lower some resistance. The rest is on you, chum."

"When?"

"Tomorrow. So I guess you won't be seeing me for a few months."

In fact, Kevin never saw the man again.

# Chapter 24

*Now*

"Well, well," Charmer said. "None the worse for wear, I see."

"No, your rapist/torturer/drug source was surprisingly gentle," Jenny replied politely.

"He'll need a trip to his own clinic," Kevin said, which nearly made her jump; he'd been so quiet on the way up, clearly lost in his own thoughts. "Had to get rough, to get him off."

"*Had* to? Again?" Charmer frowned. "Really, Kevin. There's chivalry and then there's chauvinism. Not to mention, this will make the employee picnic very awkward."

Kevin shrugged.

"Please," Charmer said, the frown vanishing to who-knew-where. "Have a seat, Miss Branch. Can I get you something? Cup of coffee? A Coke? A downer?"

"No, I'm fine." Feeling the entire situation was more than a little surreal, Jenny sat. Kevin remained standing behind her, arms crossed over his chest. "So, uh, what now?"

"Why . . . nothing." Charmer spread her hands. Jenny noticed her fingernails were brutally short, the hangnails gnawed red. Whatever Charmer might show on her face, her hands sure didn't lie. "Some of our techs are processing the information you, ah, shared with us, but the voice stress analysis looks good. Really, we're grateful."

"Grateful," Jenny said neutrally.

"Right! And we'd like to show it. Do you have, ah, any outstanding loans we can take care of for you? Perhaps a personal problem you need assistance with?"

In other words, Jenny thought, can we get you into our debt? Can we give you money so you look bad on paper and have nowhere to go? Can we ice someone for you and blackmail you into working for us?

"Gee," she said, baiting the trap, "that sounds nice, but my life is pretty okay. I make an okay living at O.S.I."

Charmer laughed, a brittle sound entirely without humor. "Oh my dear! We can do considerably better than the slave wages at O.S.I."

"You can?"

"Considerably."

"But I don't know anything else. Anything you haven't already heard, I mean. And secretaries are a dime a dozen. Why do you need me at all? I'm worthless to you."

(*Worthless bitch*)

"Miss Branch, are you *trying* to get shot in the head and dumped in a ditch?"

"Well, no," she admitted. "I just figured, you know, honesty is the best policy."

Charmer leaned forward, folding her bony hands together. Jenny resisted the urge to recommend a good cuticle cream. La Source, maybe, or something from The Body Shop.

"Worthless," Charmer said, "but that's funny, coming from you."

"Me?"

"Someone who looks like you."

"What do my *looks* have to do with anything?" she asked, honestly bewildered, as Kevin shifted his weight behind her.

Charmer flapped a hand at her. "Oh, stop it. You know. Gorgeous little blonde, big blue eyes, flawless skin, rosy cheeks—I could vomit just looking at you."

"I think *gorgeous* is a little extreme," Jenny said, thinking, *this is worse than the drug interrogation.* She could feel the hot blood rushing to her cheeks; she hated when people pretended she was prettier than she was. "And aren't we getting off topic?"

"Ugh," Charmer said, almost snarled. "You're one of those."

"Those *what*?"

"Those gorgeous women who pretend they're not gorgeous. They can look in a mirror and see plain while men are slobbering all over them."

"I have yet to encounter a slobbering man. Well, except for the good doctor downstairs. But we both know what motivates him. Your man here showed up just in time."

"Mmm. I'm just saying, if you're going to work for me, I hate your type. I think you're right—honesty is the best policy for this sort of thing."

"Well, who says I'm going to work for you?"

"You can't go back," Charmer pointed out. "Not after, how does Loman put it? Singing like a canary?"

"That does appear to be the phrase of the day," Jenny commented. "And it's not like I had a choice. He—" jerking a thumb in Kevin's direction, "—kidnapped me, and your pet psycho *doped* me before trying to feel me up. I'm definitely thinking victim, here."

"I doubt The Boss will see it that way." Charmer said it with a perfectly straight face, but couldn't keep the venom out of her tone. "He's not very trusting. Or forgiving."

*What was this about?* "Well, I—I don't have many dealings

with him in my job. As you'll probably hear yourself on the audiotape, he's just somebody who works upstairs, to me. You think everybody who works at Microsoft meets Bill Gates?"

"Mmm."

"So, uh, what do we do now? I mean, can I go? I guess that's a silly question."

A frosty smile. "I guess."

"But if I don't stay here and work . . ."

Charmer made a pistol out of her thumb and forefinger, and pointed it at Jenny.

"Oh." Jenny fought the rising nausea; this, she hadn't foreseen. "So it's not even a choice, right?"

The chilly smile widened. "Not really, dear."

"And that wasn't exactly a job offer, was it? You just brought me up here to fuck with me."

"Essentially. In fact, there might be further interrogations in your near future. Think of them as employee orientations."

"Yeah, I'm not, uh, I'm not sure I see them quite the way you do . . ."

Charmer stood—it was exactly like watching a snake uncoil—and approached Jenny, breathing closely in her ear. "If Dr. Loman is as incapacitated as most people Sidewinder roughs up, I may need to administer them myself."

"Hate to put you to all that trouble," she said weakly.

"I have to admit, I'd love a look inside that pretty little head of yours. Girls like you with low self-esteem . . . you're simply delicious."

"You're not going to—" Suddenly she was jerked to her feet.

"Done, ma'am?" Kevin rumbled.

Charmer waved them away. "Take her to holding six. See

to her restraints yourself, please—I don't think the doctor is able to tuck her in just right now. We'll start again tomorrow. Oh, and if you haven't already, call someone to fix up Loman."

"If you insist, ma'am."

# Chapter 25

"That went well," Jenny began. "But I have to say, I'm not looking forward to my follow-up with Dr. Loman. I mean, I thought the HMO doctors were bad. Is it possible that he's a grudge holder?"

"I'm sure he's forgotten all about it," Kevin replied. The elevator doors opened to a near-empty floor, which didn't surprise her. As far as she had seen, the Snakepit had very few employees, which was about right, if Charmer was half the paranoid bitch Jenny assumed she was.

Kevin nodded at a single guard and led Jenny down a hallway with the impersonal politeness of a good maitre d'. The walls on either side were clear—glass or plastic or whatever—and all the holding cells were empty.

She counted down six, and as they reached the small, bare room the glass door slid smoothly back.

"Home sweet home," Kevin said with a sarcastic smile.

"Uh-huh." She stepped inside. It was right out of *Silence of the Lambs*—bare walls, a stainless steel toilet, a bare cot. Two army blankets neatly folded on the cot. A spotless sink. No windows. "Well, I'll see you later, then."

He glanced down the hallway, then stepped closer to her. "I'm really sorry," he said in a low voice.

"For what? Sticking to the plan?" She shoved him away—that ought to look good for the cameras. He backed up a step but, annoyingly, didn't leave. "Come on, get out of here."

He started to speak again, then seemed to see the sense of her words, because he turned to leave—only to almost walk into the now-closed door.

Charmer was standing on the other side of the glass.

"Aggghh!" they said in unison.

"Don't take this the wrong way," Charmer said, "but once the trust is gone, it's very hard to rebuild the relationship."

"What the hell are you doing?" Kevin barked.

"Oh, filling the hours, you know how it goes."

"It's right nicer if you wait 'til *after* your man gets out of the cell," he said.

"Are you? My man? I'm not sure, Kevin—I have to say, I'm really not sure." Charmer tsk'ed and shook her head. "I'm interested in finding out, though. I'm simply *dying* to speak to the good doctor, but he hasn't come around yet. In the meantime, you can keep our guest company." She grinned. "I'd do it myself—I'd *love* to do it myself—but you know how it goes. All paperwork, all the time. Maybe I'll make it back down here later. Bring a bottle of white."

"Mwah-hah-hah," Jenny volunteered from the cot.

"It's almost insulting," she sniffed at him, "how dumb you think I must be."

"Dr. Loman will only be able to tell you how the lady got the drop on him."

"Oh so? Then my apologies in advance. That's the nice thing about these cells. I can open them as easily as I can close them. Don't fret, Kevin. If I've made a mistake, I'll tender a full written apology, *and* buy the beer. Not that I drink beer. But you understand. For now, there are other things to work on." She waggled bitten nails at them in a sarcastic wave. "You two have a nice evening."

"We have to share a toilet?" Jenny shouted after her. If Charmer replied, they couldn't hear it.

And then, suddenly, they were alone.

"I sense we need a new plan," she said.

"Well, fuck," Kevin snarled, obviously resisting the urge to kick the wall.

"You've had to deal with that woman for how many years?"

"Fuckfuckfuck."

"Well, they didn't take any of your guns away. Can you shoot your way out?"

"Not without the ricochets wounding or killing us. That bitch."

"That's the trouble with paranoid, evil overlord bitches," Jenny said cheerfully. "You can't trust them."

He slunk over to the cot. She was almost amused; it was obvious he had not planned to be on this side of the bars. Not that there were bars.

"How long until she comes back with the hot pokers?"

"Dunno. Depends on what Loman will tell her."

"I don't think he's going to be able to talk anytime soon." She almost giggled, remembering Kevin kicking the bad doctor around the room like a kid with a hackey sack.

"Yup, there's that." He seemed to cheer up a little. He looked at her and she marveled again at his wonderful eyes, so dark and deep, with that cute tip at the ends, making them almond-shaped and mysterious. "And there's this: I'd rather be here with you than in some fancy hotel suite without you."

She grinned. "Wait until we both have to use the toilet at the same time."

"Hush," he said, and bent to her, and kissed her.

She returned the kiss with more than polite enthusiasm, and they fell back on the cot, and she had time to mumble, "Security cameras," before he said, "Taken care of."

Then she forgot about the cameras, Charmer, Dr. Loman, The Boss, the whole mess. The only thing in this small, clean cell was Kevin, all big shoulders and long legs and their combined weight making the cot creak.

His mouth was on her mouth, her temple, her hair. He was murmuring something over and over and after a minute she was able to figure out what it was: "It's all right. Don't worry. It'll be all right."

"I'm *not* worried," she lied. "Not a bit." No, the cell didn't worry her, Charmer didn't worry her, the possibility of never seeing her home again didn't worry her, Caitlyn worrying about her didn't worry her, Mag being run by a series of temps didn't worry her, nope, nothing, *nada*.

And now it was almost true.

His hands were under her shirt and, unlike Dr. Loman's crawly touch, Kevin's was firm and welcome. She arched into him and breathed in his clean, cottony scent. He sucked her tongue into his mouth and bit lightly, and she shivered all over as if a stiff breeze was blowing through the cell.

And speaking of stiff, her fingers found his belt, delved lower; he was like cloth-covered stone, and they writhed together on the cot for a moment, trying to give each other access without tearing anything.

She reached, groped, steadied a hand on the wall as he unzipped her jeans, pushed clothing aside, undid his own pants, shoved inside her. She groaned on the downstroke and he shuddered over her like a man with a fever, and for a moment neither of them moved.

Then he shifted and she arched, and they met each other

again and again under the harsh fluorescent lights, making the cot creak, forcing gasps from each other.

Will I be dead in an hour? she thought. Is that why I'm doing this crazy thing? He could be knocking me up right now. He could be giving me V.D. He could—

—be making her come, be making things around the edges go dark, be whispering in her hair and touching her face, be forcing her legs wider to accommodate him, all of him, be shuddering and whispering her name.

Be still.

He was resting his forehead on her shoulder, breathing hard. She reached, found the back of his neck, stroked it.

"That'll teach Charmer to lock us up," she said, and he started laughing so hard he almost fell off the cot.

# Chapter 26

"So now what?" she whispered.

He got off her, pulled her shirt down, helped her up. Looked away politely as she zipped and tucked. Arranged his own clothes.

"Now we get the fu—the heck out of Dodge." He took out his wallet, took out a stiff card and some small metal things, stepped up on the cot, fiddled around for a moment with his arms over his head, and pulled a square off the ceiling.

She gaped; did all the cells come with handy hidden fuse boxes? Or whatever was up in the ceiling? Not a fuse box, something else, something only a Snakepit employee would be able to find quickly and—

She didn't hear it, but sensed it, and turned; the door was sliding open.

"I'm not mad or anything," she said, "but why didn't you do that ten minutes ago?"

He gave her a look. "I had other things on my mind."

"Mmmm." She couldn't decide if she was annoyed or flattered.

"Come on." He took her by the hand, led her out, led her down the dark hall—among other things, he'd done something to the lights—and seemed unsurprised to see the guard was not at his desk. "Let's blow."

"Blow as in leave? Or are we going to participate in the secret sexual Olympics again?"

"Hush."

"Sorry, I'm a little nervous, and I babble when I'm nervous."

"You've never babbled in your life." He opened the door to the stairwell. "Time to get those little legs of yours moving."

"Had enough fun in the Pit for one day, huh?"

"I decided *that*," he said, leading the way down the stairwell, "when I saw Loman on the floor."

"We're just going to leave? Just like that?"

"Yup."

"Now?"

"Yup."

"But won't somebody see us?"

"Prob'ly."

She stopped in midstep. "There's got to be a better way to do this."

He turned around. "Come on, Jenn."

She fought the urge to stamp her foot. Oh, for nanobytes in her bloodstream right about now! She'd boot him down the stairwell, go back, and break Charmer's neck.

"Kevin. Come on. I'm a receptionist and I know this won't work. We don't even have a contingency plan for this!" *Cripes*, why didn't we have a contingency plan for this?

"I'm not leaving you in a fu—in a cage."

"Well, we can't just leave right this second without a plan. Leave me in a cage for a while, find Charmer and plead your case, make her believe you're still one of them. Just don't forget to come get me." She realized what she had said and, stricken, added, "I'm sorry. I didn't mean that how it sounded. I know you'd never leave anyone behind."

He smiled at her, a real smile, not like Charmer's grimaces. "Don't fret, sweetie. Besides, I wouldn't say there ain't a plan."

# Chapter 27

They emerged from the building and Jenny was struck silent, stopped still, and stared.

"No time for sight-seeing." Kevin was busy doing something with the door—he had produced what looked like a dull-gray credit card and ran it through the small metal ID box, the kind that looked like credit-card machines. Instead of "Entrance granted" or "$35.16" or whatever, "XXXXXXXX" flashed in green letters on the tiny screen. She heard a clank as the door locked itself.

"This—we're—the Snakepit's—"

"In the Iowa State Fairgrounds," he confirmed. "Sure. Who'd look for us here? Fifty weeks a year this place is deader than sh—than heck."

Still she goggled: she could see the giant, two-story yellow slide, various shut-up booths

(*Cheese Curds! Sno-Kones! Foot-Longs!*) and the Got Milk? booth.

*Got Spies?* she thought wildly.

"Come on," he said, and took her hand. "We need to stay off the midway. Stick to the little side streets. This time of night, there's hardly anybody around. Most of 'em are in the main building, but we gotta watch out for booby traps."

"She set up the Snakepit at the state fair? And then booby-trapped the midway?" What a perversion of all that was good! Jenny could hardly believe it. Oooh, that Charmer was a brass bitch, and that was for sure. A brass bitch who needed highlights and a manicure in the worst way. And Jenny didn't even want to *think* about what that woman's feet must need. "But that's so wrong!"

"We'll talk about it later."

"I can't believe we got out. Was that too easy?"

"Easy? She calls that easy?" He smiled at her. "But to your point: I'm not surprised we got out. I am a professional, after all. And I have a pretty charmer by my side."

"A pretty tired charmer," she replied. "Wait. Don't call me that."

"Come on." He caught her hand and they moved off, deeper into the fairgrounds.

Before she could lend a hand, or duck, he'd shoved her behind the cow-and-sheep barn and taken out the small border patrol. She heard the dull thuds and cracks and winced, hoping he wasn't killing anyone. She peeked just in time to see the third man drop.

Carrying them fireman-style, he dumped the men back in the Jeep. She crept over and saw all their communications equipment was dark; nothing was in the red, nothing was lit.

"Excellent," he grunted.

"What?"

"I took some time to leave a few surprises in the basement."

"So the bad guys are losing power?" she guessed.

"Among other things. I suppose Charmer was right not to trust me, eh?"

"When did you do that?"

"Before my chess game with Charmer, she had me running a few errands around the complex. Enough time to, well, shift about the ordnance inventory, so to speak. I had to do something to pass the time during your date with Dr. Loman, after all."

"So you always meant for us to leave sooner rather than later?"

He shrugged. "I move a bit faster than your boss probably imagines. The time in the cell was the only delay I didn't expect. Hop in."

"Finally! I thought we were going to walk all over these fairgrounds."

"We can ride for a bit. I gotta get this Jeep outta sight."

She gingerly climbed over one of the men (who was bleeding unattractively from one ear) and settled in the passenger seat. "I have to say, I'm having the weirdest couple of days."

"You'll get used to it."

"That's what I'm afraid of."

# Chapter 28

"Why didn't we keep the Jeep?" she asked.

"Shhhh." They were crouched behind the Seed and Nursery building and, as the sun went down, Jenny was finding it harder and harder to see in the deepening gloom. At least it was off-season. Or maybe that was a bad thing. If it had been fair season, after all, they could have disappeared into a crowd of a hundred thousand people. But as it was, the two of them had to be sticking out.

Worse, on foot, they didn't feel comfortable using flashlights, or even the glow of his cell phone screen.

"You should have brought some night-vision goggles in that utility belt of yours," she mumbled.

"Shhhh."

"Why didn't we keep the Jeep?" she whispered. "We'll need a car when we get to the gates."

"Too conspicuous."

"As opposed to creeping across the fairgrounds like a couple of fruitcakes who've seen too many Bond movies."

"Come on." He took her by the wrist and pulled her to her feet.

"Don't think I haven't noticed how you ignore me when I've come up with something unanswerable."

"I didn't hear that, either."

They darted past the Nursery, the gyros-and-calzones booth, Beef Promotions of Iowa, Chicken Strips, Smoothies, and Funnel Cakes. Jenny's sensation that she was in a dream deepened. It wasn't possible for the day to get any more—

"Move!"

Headlights splashed menacingly across the pork rinds booth and they both ducked, but there was nowhere to go. Either the driver saw their flattened shapes upon the pavement, or didn't. Fortunately, they caught a break as the Jeep zoomed on.

"They aren't even looking for us yet?" she asked with total disbelief.

"Charmer's probably calling everybody to the main building. I left a lot of goodies for her to sort through. She's got her hands full." Satisfaction seeped from his voice, not that she could blame him. She'd only known Charmer for half a day; what must it have been like for him? Pretending to be a member of the team while trying not to puke, or belt someone.

"How'd you make it for four years?" she couldn't help asking.

He gave her a look. "You'd be surprised what you can put up with when there's no choice."

"You're telling someone who lives through Minnesota winters about putting up with stuff?"

He snickered. "Yup, there's that. When we get out of here, we're going to Southern Pines."

"We are, huh? What's in Southern Pines?"

"The best fishing in the state of North Carolina, and that's just for a start. Let's hit it," he said, and took her wrist again, and off they went.

# Chapter 29

"**I**'m sorry," she panted, "I've got to rest."

"Okay."

"It's just that it's so big. It seems like we've been running forever." Running, ducking, pausing, running again, hiding, running, as quietly as they could. It wasn't so much the physical exertion as trying to exert herself without making any noise. Purely exhausting.

She remembered telling The Boss that this was her movie, not Dmitri's, not Caitlyn's. Too bad now. Those two would have run circles around the fairgrounds, and probably would have knocked over the main building with their bare hands. Pulled Charmer's limbs off like a kid torturing a fly.

She was alarmed at how much the thought pleased her.

At least it wasn't raining. As far as she could tell, it had been a pretty nice day. Too bad she'd spent it all inside.

"Five minutes," he said. Then he cocked his head just as she heard the sounds of approach. He stood up and hit the door of the small building with his shoulder; it practically popped off the hinges (*two hundred twenty pounds times force times velocity . . . wait, that's not right . . .*) and they went inside. It was as black as jeweler's velvet, and Jenny hesitated a little. Walking inside a strange, small building that may or may not have a step when she couldn't see her hand in front of her face was too creepy. Then she heard a click, and Kevin was shining a small penlight around the building—really more like a shack.

"Cripes!" he almost yelled, and she jumped. After an hour of whispering, it was startling, to say the least.

"What?" She looked around wildly; suddenly every shadowy corner seemed extra sinister—she could practically see armed men crouching, hiding, ready to grab. "Is someone in here? What?"

"This is the Snakepit!"

"What?" He had, she assumed, cracked under the pressure (poor guy). Then she took a look around, and saw all the paintings of snakes on the walls.

"Okay," she said, trying to calm herself—her heart felt like it was pumping in her throat. "You scared the shit out of me. So we're in the Reptile House. It's fine. As long as there's nobody else in here with us."

"This is where they keep the cobras and the rattlers and the cottonmouths." In the poor glow of the penlight, he looked positively green. "Ugh!"

"Kevin, calm down. It's off-season—there aren't any snakes in here at all."

"Maybe one got away. Maybe it's lurking in the dark ready to bite our feet—"

"You're afraid of snakes? You?"

"They wait," he said, and she could hear how his voice shook. She had to think about bullets and Dr. Loman and Charmer's hands to keep from laughing. "They bite in the dark."

"Shhh. Keep your voice down. Come over here, sit down.

Give me that." She took the flashlight, led him to the corner, and they sat on the floor. She could hear a Jeep engine humming and thrumming in the area; the walls were thin enough so she could hear the guards talking to each other, but couldn't make out what they were saying. A routine patrol? Something else?

"They bite in the dark," he was still muttering, twisting to look behind his ankles.

"So does the I.R.S.," she confided. "I feel the same way about them."

"I just—hate them. They give me the fu—the creeps. They're not like a dog. You can't train 'em."

"You never heard the old 'they're more scared of you than you are of them' thing?"

"That," he replied, "would be impossible."

She took his hand, which was cold, and rubbed the knuckles. "We won't stay here long," she soothed. "Just until the patrol leaves."

He shuddered and didn't answer.

"Thanks for getting me out," she whispered.

"I got you in," he said after a long pause. "Don't be thanking me for that."

"Still. It was my idea to go, you know. It was my idea to ask you to come back. I guess neither of us did the other any favors."

He laughed, muffling the sound against the back of his hand. The hand she was holding, in fact. His breath tickled her fingers. Then he stiffened. "Did you hear that?" he whispered. "Like . . . a slithering?"

"I don't know what slithering sounds like, but I'm sure there isn't anything in here but us. Maybe a few mice."

"They eat mice."

"Yes, but their handlers took them all away last year. And

even if they didn't, the snakes would be behind the glass. We're out here."

"Like we were behind glass a little while ago?"

"Okay, that's not the same thing at all," she said patiently. "You are not a boa constrictor. Humans can pick locks. Snakes cannot."

"They can get into real small spaces."

"Speaking of small spaces, are we really going to sit here in the dark and worry about snakes, or are you going to kiss me?"

"Uh. Well."

"Dope," she said, and found his face, and pulled it to her, and kissed him for a lovely, long time. He was tense in her arms at first—it was like kissing a wooden idol. Listening for the elusive slither, no doubt. But after a few seconds he loosened up, his arms came around her, his tongue stroked her lower lip, and she heard a roaring in her ears that could have been a posse of snakes sneaking up on them, or a pride of lions, but she didn't give a rat's ass.

He tasted clean and strong, like well water, like cotton, and (how was this for sick, she asked herself) the light scent of gun oil was making her seriously horny.

*Don't be silly, you're just cracking under the pressure, just like in the cell, grabbing a little life while you've got a little life.*

*So?*

So, indeed. She opened her mouth for him, clutched at him, groped at him, and he squeezed her so tightly she gasped.

"Bad idea," she managed as his fingers lifted her shirt, settled over her pounding heart, caressed the sensitive flesh just outside her bra cups.

His hands withdrew at once. "I'm sorry," he whispered. "You're right. I don't know what I was thinkin'. Bad enough I jumped you in the cell, especially after Dr. Loman—"

"Him? I wasn't even thinking about him. And don't you

dare apologize for what happened earlier. I wanted it as much as you did." Possibly more than you did, she thought but did not say. "I was thinking about birth control. I wasn't worried about it before, when death loomed, but now I'm pretty sure we've got a good chance to fight another day. And the thing is, I don't have any."

"Well, I got good news, maybe."

"Yeah?"

"I had rubella when I was a kid."

"Sterile, huh?"

"No babies for me," he agreed in a low voice. "No ladies for me, either, not for a long time. The cell was the first time in—I mean, I never wanted nobody at the Pit, so—"

She thought of a line from an Andrew Vachs book. "So you went steady with your fist?"

He snorted. "Funny thing is, I always thought it was a good thing. Never wanted a kid to worry about, the life I lead. But then—I mean, the last few days—"

"Stop it," she said, "I'm blushing."

"I can't tell in the dark."

She brought his hand to her face. "See? Don't I feel hot to you?'

"Yup," he agreed, and kissed her again.

"Bad idea," she mumbled into his mouth.

"Yup."

"And if we did anything, we'd have to be really, really quiet."

"Yup."

"And it's stupid. I can't think of a worse time or place."

"Yup."

"You'd think we got it out of our system earlier."

"Yup."

"But, you know. As long as we're stuck in here."

"To pass the time," he said between kisses. His lips

pressed against her mouth, her chin, her brow. "You're so beautiful, Jenn. You're the most beautiful woman I ever saw."

"I'm really not," she said, and put his hand where it belonged: over her heart.

# Chapter 30

He forgot about the snakes. This was a minor miracle, because if there was one thing in the world he fucking hated, it was those slithering, cold, slimy, disgusting reptiles. And never mind all the irony about ending up in the Snakepit, either. One thing didn't have anything to do with the other.

But who cared? Jenny was beneath his hands, squirming toward his touch; Jenny was breathing so hard she was gasping, her skin like velvet against his, her hair like rough silk. Her breasts filled his hands, the nipples stiffening against his palms, and his mouth actually watered; he had to taste her again, taste her where he was touching her, suckle her smooth skin.

Had he thought the time in the cell was good? Death and sex and all that shit all tangled up in his head, and had he thought that was good? This was better. Nobody was looking over their shoulder in here. It was just him and her and her softness, her sweetness.

She was whispering in the dark, running restless fingers through his hair, rubbing the back of his neck. Her shirt and bra were around her neck and she was wriggling around to help him pull her jeans down. In the small shack, their breathing was very loud—it was the world, *she* was the world.

He found her mouth again, parted her lips with his tongue, smelled her sweet breath, nibbled on her lower lip. He wanted to eat her like a nectarine, touch her everywhere, lick and kiss and suck, and he'd never wanted anyone more. His cock throbbed; it felt like there was a brick in his pants.

She was grabbing for him, touching him, stroking him right through his fatigues, and the throbbing intensified; his head spun, and he managed to pull her hands away from him. "Don't," he groaned, "oh, don't. We'll be done before we start."

"So start," she whispered back, fingers busy at his fly, tongue flicking at his ear. "And you should know that, under the circumstances, speed is a good thing."

He laughed into her mouth, groped, cupped her ass, her sweet, smooth ass. God, what a butt on the woman—it didn't matter where you looked at her, she was just too damned fine.

He found her zipper, pulled it down, slipped his hand inside. Found panties he couldn't see but imagined they were white or pink.

He was embarrassed to admit to himself he hadn't looked before, had been in such a damn hurried rush, all he'd cared about was getting inside her, getting as close to her as he could. And now when he could look, it was too damned dark. So he imagined. Yup, pink. He loved pink panties; he was a pig who loved pink on a woman, pink like Jenny's cheeks, pink like her panties, which may or may not have been pink. They could have had orange elephants on them, for all he could tell.

He slipped his fingers past the elastic, savored the silky hair beneath his hand, slipped his fingers inside and found her wet and slick and ready, either from what he was doing or from before, he didn't care which. What mattered was she was ready for him—God, she was ready, thank God, thank God.

She'd pulled and tugged and was holding him; God, she was actually *holding his dick* in her small, sweet hands, and they were practically wrestling on the floor, each trying to give the other more access, and she was guiding him, touching him and wriggling to give him room. He slid into her and it was so quick and sweet, he was in her to the hilt before his brain knew what was happening.

"Ah," she said, and he found her mouth in the dark, kissed her, devoured her.

For a long moment he didn't move, couldn't move; if he moved, it would be over sooner and he never wanted it to be over, never. And if he started, he would pound her like a nail, and he wanted it to be as amazing for her as it was for him. Women were refined creatures, they needed more than the old slam and bam; surely he could make it last at least half a minute longer than last time.

But she wasn't having it—she was squirming beneath him and he thought his head was going to explode, just blow up like a bald tire.

He slid against her, stroked, and her hips rose to meet his; her heels were pressed against the backs of his calves, her small teeth were nibbling at his ear which was really making him nuts, and he was thrusting and groping and thinking *God, God, don't hurt her, take it easy, she's little, you've got fifty pounds on her at least, last time was last time but this time there's no excuse*, but his body was ignoring him, his dick was in the driver's seat, and thank God she didn't seem to mind the ride.

The noises she was making, ah God, such sweet little

purring sounds, and the tiny part of his brain that was still functioning thought, *noise*, and he covered her lips with his palm, and then she licked his palm and then his head *did* blow up.

Or at least, that's what it felt like.

# *Chapter 31*

"Nobody came in and blew our heads off," she whispered.

He groaned softly in reply. He'd sort of collapsed over her, which was flattering, if suffocating.

"At least, I'm pretty sure. I *feel* like my head's been blown off."

"Tell me," he said, and pulled away. They readjusted themselves in the dark, and the silence should have been weird and awkward, but wasn't.

"Do you think it's safe to go out?"

"The patrol left about two minutes ago."

"Always the soldier," she teased in a whisper.

"No," he said in a low voice. "Not always."

She groped in the dark, found his shirt, clutched it. "If I never get a chance to tell you, I'll tell you now: thank you."

"You're thanking *me*?" he asked, and in his surprise he forgot to lower his voice.

"Shhhh! Yes, I'm thanking you—what, I should be hitting you instead? I shouldn't thank you for the best sex ever? Again?"

"It has been? It has been," he replied, answering his own

question. "I mean, I know how it's been for me, but every time it seems so fast—"

"In case you haven't noticed, I'm a quick study."

He smiled, she was pretty sure. It was so damn dark! "Yeah. I noticed."

"It was kind of dumb, though."

"I'm sorry," he said immediately.

"I guess I shouldn't have molested you like that, here with the snakes."

"Uh—"

"Not that I haven't been dying to. But time and place, you know? Luckily this is my non-movie, and as the non-star, nothing too bad will happen to me."

"Okay," he said, sounding as if he doubted her sanity but was too polite to ask questions.

*I love you*, she thought. *Since I took your gun away in the men's room. Since you let me. Since you held me in the cell and told me everything was going to be all right. No, before that. That just made me love you more. And I didn't think I could love you more. And how's that for crazy?*

"So . . ." Her voice sounded odd to her ears, so she cleared her throat and tried again. "What now?"

"We hit the bricks again."

She sighed. "No nap, huh? That's the worst news I've had all day. I could really use a nap."

"I promise. You'll get your nap. Later."

"Just a nap?" she teased. "At least we don't need to waste time condom-shopping. I'm not riddled with disease or anything, by the way. In case you were wondering."

"Frankly, the thought never crossed my mind."

She almost laughed. "Men."

"You hush. Seducing me like that, then giving me shit. Ought to be shamed."

"Oooooh, you said *shit* to a lady."

"Long day."

She carefully stood, keeping her balance by touching the wall. Her bra was riding up like a living, contrary thing and she adjusted it. He stayed where he was, sitting on the floor.

"You remembered I told you I had rubella when I was a kid?"

"It was five minutes ago, so . . . yes. Why, is this the part where you tell me it was a lie your dick convinced you to tell?"

He didn't take offense. "No. It's true. I remember it real well, because it was the last Christmas I was able to think of my daddy as a smart man. Next Christmas, I was already trying to figure out how things could turn out different for me. I was different, too. That was the last Christmas I felt like a member of the family."

"I'm sorry," she said at once. "That's pretty bad."

"Well." He sounded slightly embarrassed. "I just wanted to say."

"I'm glad you said. I guess you miss them. You haven't seen them in all this time—"

"I went undercover to get away from them."

"I can relate. I don't miss mine."

"Liar," he said, and she bit her lip to stop the tears.

# Chapter 32

"All that I thought was good and decent has been perverted," she commented, watching him crack the lock to the Funhouse.

"You have to admit, it's a real good idea. Who'd ever look here for the Snakepit?"

"I was talking about sex in the Reptile House, but breaking into the Funhouse to check on the bad guys is right up there."

"It's one of the few hot spots I didn't blow up," he said, as if that was a perfectly reasonable explanation. "I just want to check on their progress, scope the rest of the park."

"It seems like we've been in this place for hours."

"We have."

"That explains it, then."

She followed him inside, and when the door clanked shut behind them, he did something to the metal box in the entryway and suddenly the place was flooded with light.

She saw a petite blonde staring at her and almost screeched. Then realized there were twenty petite blondes, and twenty Kevins.

"Fucking Funhouse mirrors," she muttered.

"That's no way for a lady to talk," he teased.

"I'm on the ragged edge, here. The fun drained out of this little party about half an hour ago."

He didn't reply (what was there to say?), so she followed him through the mirrors, past the zigzag walls, and ducked as they went into a tunnel painted in wavy pastel shades.

"I've mentioned the general perversion of innocence, right?" she asked, more to hear herself talk than anything else. It was creepy in here, and that was a fact.

He didn't answer, perhaps sensing that she was talking to herself rather than him. He stepped up a small set of wiggling stairs, hit a spot on the wall, and flipped the wooden strongman cutout around, revealing a small bank of cameras and several switches.

"It's safe to have the lights on?"

"No windows leading to the outside," he replied absently, squinting at the cameras. "Six of one, half-dozen of th'other if the lights are on or off."

"Oh."

He blinked and said, surprised, "It doesn't look like anybody's looking for us."

"Maybe they're all in the main building. Having an evil conference, or whatever."

"Maybe." He clearly had his doubts. "There's a routine patrol on the south end—we can avoid them easily enough. But the guards are missing from the north gate."

"Trap?"

"Maybe."

"You said you were keeping them busy. Maybe they're trying to get things built back up."

"Yeah, there's only a couple dozen of us. Kinda what I was counting on. It just seems a little too neat, doesn't it?"

"Perhaps," she said, "but you've been one step ahead of them so far."

"Yup, I s'pose. Nothing to brag on for me, though—they

aren't used to any kind of resistance, never mind one of their own causing trouble. Charmer keeps everybody in line."

"I'm sure." She added, "And you were never one of them."

That seemed to please him; at least, he smiled. "Let's make tracks sooner rather than later."

She followed him back through the silly tunnel and the maze of mirrors (she saw her messy hair and dirty blouse, times twenty). Kevin was practically bouncing along, pulling her by the hand and humming some song under his breath. After a minute, she placed it: "Who Let the Dogs Out."

"We can move a lot faster now," he said, immensely cheered. "We'll be past the border by sunup."

"Iowa: land of evil splinter cells. Who would have thought I'd be so glad to see the rural border metropolis of Albert Lea?"

"This whole day's been 'who would have thought.'"

"You have a point there, dearest."

He snorted. "Dearest."

"Dearest darling? Honey? Sweetie-pie? Darling? Sugar-lump? Noogums?"

"Never, ever that last one."

"Okay, fair enough."

He popped the lights back off and they emerged into the cool summer dark. Hand in hand, they moved past the Iowan Tourism building, the 4-H barns, the show rings, the agriculture building, the—

"Wait," Kevin said, at almost the exact same time that a brittle voice came from the shadows of the Swine Barn.

"You didn't really think you had gotten away from me, did you?"

# Chapter 33

Kevin already had his gun out and Jenny was groping herself to find a weapon, any weapon—maybe she could pull a button off her blouse and sharpen it? Throw her shoe? Fart?

"Better not, Charmer. It's just easier to let us go."

"Easier than what?"

"Than getting shot."

"You're assuming I don't have ten people pointing guns at you right now."

"Yeah," he said. "I'm assuming that."

Charmer stepped out where they could see her. "For the record, I have been tracking you since your escape from the cell."

"All part of your sinister plan, huh?" Jenny asked.

"Well, yes."

"And you just—let it all happen?"

"Well, yes."

"All right then, how did you get in front of us?"

"I took a Jeep, idiot."

"Oh."

"Don't you want to know how I knew where you were going?"

Jenny set her mind to it and figured it out, her heart—galloping briskly in her chest from the fright—starting to slow a bit. "I assume you have some secret minicams that Kevin couldn't get to, or didn't blow up."

Charmer looked disappointed. "Well, yes."

Kevin holstered his gun. Charmer seemed indifferent, but Jenny relaxed a little. Apparently there would be no shooting. That was fine. It had been a long damn day and she wasn't in the mood to dodge bullets. Though she wouldn't mind seeing Charmer dodge a few.

"So what happens now?" he asked.

"You kidnap me, use me for safe passage out of the grounds, and bring me back to O.S.I."

Jenny looked at Kevin, who was looking at her. They both looked at Charmer, who was shifting her weight from foot to foot as she waited for their answer. She'd changed from her severe suit to black pants and a black turtleneck. Black tennis shoes. Her hair was pulled back, making her narrow face seem almost skull-like in the gloom.

"You *want* to be kidnapped?" Jenny finally asked.

"Look who's talking!"

"But—you want to go with us?"

"You *want* to get home without being perforated by various rifles?"

"But—why?"

"Change of scenery?" Charmer suggested.

"Come on, Charmer. What are you really up to?"

"What?" She managed to sound wounded and almost—but not quite—innocent. "I can't keep secret tabs on you as you betray me and escape, follow you and give myself up, without you making a big thing about it?"

"Cripes," Kevin muttered. He turned to Jenny. "You realize it's some sort of elaborate trick."

"I assumed," she replied.

"So we take her with us or we don't."

"I'm really curious about what happens next," she admitted. "So let's take her."

"That's the spirit!" Charmer said.

"Shut up. She could see that things have gone bad. She's crazy, but not dumb."

"You're half right," Charmer said cheerfully.

They ignored her. "You're saying," Kevin said, "this might be her way out—leave somebody else holding the bag while she beats feet for the hills?"

"I would *never*."

"Shut up."

"She's let us get this far," Jenny said.

"Yup, she did."

"The operative word," Charmer couldn't resist saying, "being *let*."

"You said yourself this was all a little too easy. Let's just cuff her, bring her along, and see what she's up to."

"I can hear everything, you know."

"Shut up," they said in unison.

# Chapter 34

The walk to the exit was smooth sailing. Charmer plodded along behind them, still sulking after Kevin had frisked her. The moon was out. There was a light breeze in the air, and since all the animals were gone, the breeze was actually pleasant.

"You snuck all the way out here and couldn't have brought your Jeep?" Jenny asked at one point.

"And have Stone panic and shoot out the tires when I got too close? I can't handle that kind of stress at my age."

"You're about *my* age," Kevin commented.

"Well, then, maybe you shouldn't try to handle that level of stress, either," Charmer said cheerfully. "How are you driving back to O.S.I.?"

"Uh—"

"We're not *walking* all the way to Minneapolis?" she asked sharply.

"Look, this is freaking me out a little. You're supposed to be shooting at us or giving orders to someone to shoot at us or watching us leave on a monitor and cursing us."

"Or muddling around in the chaos of blown-up circuitry and such in the main building, shouting useless orders as we make our escape," Jenny added.

"Right," Kevin said. "Not hopping along for the ride and asking what the plan is."

"I told you," she said, sounding wounded. "You're kidnapping me. None of this is my idea."

"You're really nuts," Jenny said. "Or you're a psychopathic liar. Either way: bad guy."

"*Nuts* is in the eye of the beholder. And you didn't answer my question. How are we getting to Minneapolis?"

"I'll cross that bridge later."

Jenny thought about it. He'd either made plans to rendezvous with someone, stashed a car, or had plans to steal one.

The first choice was unlikely, as he couldn't have known when he'd escape. The second option was also unlikely, as a member of the Snakepit could have found the empty vehicle and asked embarrassing questions. So it was probably the third. She hoped he had a plan to avoid incarceration for grand theft auto.

"Fine," Charmer was pouting, "don't tell me."

"I won't," he replied, sounding aggrieved. She couldn't blame him. The whole thing was beyond bizarre.

"Gates," Charmer said. "Sadly, the men who usually guard this entrance were diverted."

"That *is* sad. What are you up to? Are you a double agent, too?"

"A traitor to my team, you mean?"

"Double agent," Kevin said sharply.

"You promised to obey my orders and fulfill any needs the organization needed," Charmer reminded him. "Which was a lie. What's worse, showing up planning to lie and desert, or changing your mind halfway, and then deserting?"

"Oh, knock it off," Jenny snapped. "You're running an insane asylum whose residents run around destroying and hijacking and raping, so don't go all wounded and sanctimonious. Let's get one thing straight: Kevin and I are the good guys. *You're* the bad guy."

"Semantics," she sniffed.

The gate was unlocked, just adding to the general surreal situation. There was a hybrid SUV idling in the distance, and as they stepped into the pool of light cast by the lone streetlight, the vehicle revved up, screeched in reverse, and shuddered to a stop four feet from Kevin.

The window slid down and Jenny was shocked to see Dmitri in the driver's seat, Caitlyn waving at them from the passenger side. "What are you waiting for?" she cried. "Hop in, dopes!"

They hopped. There was plenty of room in the back for the three of them to sit abreast.

"Did you know we can home in on your cell phone signal, even when it's off?" Dmitri asked in a 'did you know it might not rain tomorrow' tone of voice.

Jenny laughed. "I knew I hung around you guys for a reason."

"So," Caitlyn said brightly. Jenny noticed that in the day she'd been gone, her friend had dyed her hair from dark red to platinum. "Who's your little friend?"

# Chapter 35

"This is extremely weird," Caitlyn said, running her ID through the box and waiting for the elevator. "We send Jenn and Kevin off to the Pit to get intel, Jenny poses as someone with access to info they want, and now you bring back someone for us to interrogate."

"Is that your job?" Charmer asked with poisonous sweetness. "To recap?"

Dmitri smothered a laugh, earning a withering look from his wife. "What's interesting is the lady seems to be telling the truth. Her vitals are like rocks."

"You must be one of the cyborgs," Charmer said. "We've been looking for you—even a photo of you—for years."

"Please," Dmitri said, courteously allowing her to precede him into the elevator. "I prefer the term nano-enhanced."

"Whatever you're up to, Charmer, the jig's about up," Jenny said. "Don't you want to tell us before we drag it out of you?"

"No."

"No Dr. Loman in this place," Kevin added as the doors slid shut and the elevator slid smoothly upward. "But we can still be persuasive."

Charmer paused in the hallway, making them all wait for

her. "Sidewinder—can I still call you Sidewinder?—you haven't persuaded me of a damn thing in four years. Including what you've always been up to."

Kevin didn't say anything in response. His face turned gray, and Jenny and everyone else understood why from the start: his mission four years ago had been for nothing, since he had never fooled the people he thought he had fooled.

"Jesus," he whispered. "Guess I'm not the smart one in the family after all."

She felt her cheeks flush as Charmer turned to her.

"And you. What's *your* story? Newly recruited into the O.S.I., a fresh, young piece of ass who desires adventure, a Jennifer Garner wannabe? Obviously you're not a run-of-the-mill secretary."

Jenny slapped the bitch. She couldn't help herself— Charmer had hurt Kevin, and made him waste four years of his life. It was almost shameful, how good it felt. Charmer's head shot to the side and Jenny's palm went numb. She didn't care if her hand fell off. Nothing had ever felt so good. "No secretary is run-of-the-mill, you whore!"

"Ladies, ladies," Dmitri said with a small smile. Jenn noticed he made no move to stop her, though he could have, easily. All of them could have stopped her, for that matter.

Even Charmer, which was something to think about.

"Last chance to talk, Charmer," Caitlyn said as the doors opened, revealing the executive floor.

"For what? Don't talk to me, you bleached freak."

"Hey!" Caitlyn said sharply. "I am not *bleached*. The color you see is a sampling of high-quality highlights and a mixture of—"

"And she's not a freak, either," Jenny said loyally.

"You took the words right out of my mouth," Dmitri said, his mouth gone thin with dislike. "What a pity to be relieved of your company, Charmer."

"What's it like being a zombie run by machines?" Charmer asked with what appeared to be honest curiosity. "Aren't you supposed to be dead?"

"I bet all the boys were crazy about you in school," Caitlyn said. "With your split ends that matched your personality, and all that."

Charmer opened her mouth to respond, but closed it as Dmitri waved his palm in front of the sensory device on the wall and the door slid open, revealing a small front office, which was empty.

As if there had been a truce, the five of them silently walked through the small office and into the larger executive suite. Kevin still looked like he might throw up, and his hand was straying dangerously close to his sidearm, but he seemed to be keeping a lid on things, for which Jenny was grateful, and admiring.

The Boss was waiting for them. When he saw Charmer his eyes narrowed and his grip tightened on the coffee cup, but he said nothing.

"Hi, Dad," she said. "It's great to see you again, you fucking asshole from hell."

# Chapter 36

*Father issues!* Jenny couldn't get over it. It was an hour later, she was in Kevin's safe house, it was all over, and she still couldn't get over it.

The Snakepit had been a sort of twisted therapy of sorts, the Charmer had revealed to them in the brief moments she had before The Boss had shooed the rest of them out of his office. Jenny couldn't catch the exact details—but it didn't matter.

Whether she was trying to prove something to herself, or to him, or just following a conscience gone insane in an attempt to heal herself from some slight in her youth, she had caused untold devastation through her misapplied genius.

And now she had come home, when it all fell apart. Just like so many children do, when things go wrong and they have nowhere else to turn.

Jenny stopped her furious pacing in the cramped living room and turned to Kevin. "I just can't believe it!"

"Sweetie, I know. You've been saying." Kevin was sprawled on the couch, watching her with a grin.

"Why would she come back home? Why would she think she could come back? It's ridiculous! She'll be in jail the rest of her life, and her father will still hate her! The hell?"

"It's a mystery, all right," he agreed.

She whirled on him. "Isn't this bugging the hell out of you?"

"Honey, I'm just glad to be out." He swung his booted feet up onto the ready-to-crack coffee table. "The tech weenies are going over the discs I took out, *we're* out. And I'm glad you're okay. The rest is just—shit."

*Shee-yit.* It was funny how his drawl deepened when he talked to her. So soothing. She could listen to him swear all day. *Awl thayat fuckin' boo-ull shee-yit don' mean crayp. Just yer tits 'n' ass, honeybuns. That's all Ah need.* She stifled a hee-hee and plopped down on the couch beside him.

"Don't get me wrong," she said, "I'm glad we're safe. It just seems—I don't know. Like she should be dead. Or we should. With all of us alive, it's so . . . anticlimactic."

"That's a good thing," he said, kneading the back of her neck with one hand. "Trust me. And you did real great for your first time out."

"That's just it. I didn't do anything."

He stared at her. "What are you, kiddin' me? You conned your way in, beat the shit out of their pet rapist, kept your head, and got my mind off poisonous snakes."

She waved the praise away. "Anything sounds good when you add poisonous snakes."

"Honey, I was pretty proud to be workin' with you."

"Is that what you call it?" she teased. "*Working* with you? What, we're co-workers? Colleagues at the office?"

He didn't smile. Just looked straight at her with those dark eyes. "I sure hope we're more than that after everything."

"Kevin . . ." *I love you. Isn't that silly? I barely know you. But I can't imagine life without you.*

"You're a woman in a billion, Jenny Branch. A zillion."

"Yup, Ah sure am," she said, aping his laid-back accent.

Finally, he laughed. "That was more Foghorn Leghorn than a real Southern boy."

"Oooh, stop talking about cartoon chickens—it gets me hot."

"Yeah?" He had stopped rubbing her neck, was now running his fingers through her tangled hair. "You know what I could use, honey?"

"A Big Mac?" she guessed.

He looked distracted for a moment. "That does sound good. But I was thinking *a shower*."

She smiled at him. "What a coincidence. I was just thinking about how dirty I felt."

# Chapter 37

Hot water beat down on them as he soaped her thoroughly, washed her hair (it wasn't a salon product, but she didn't want to break the mood by complaining), rinsed it, washed it again.

She rubbed the soap all over his sleekly muscled body, marveling at the scars—a few knife nicks, one bullet, old road rash. A life on the run and, later—well, one way or another, he'd been running from his family since he'd been a child. She didn't have the details, but could make some educated guesses.

She even remembered reading about Kevin's father and brothers. The Stone family crime syndicate. Thugs who were successful in spite of themselves. Mafia Clouseaus. She'd find out more on the Internet, later, when he wasn't soaping her breasts.

She ran slippery fingers over his shoulders, down his back, over his butt. She lathered up still more and cupped his testicles, rubbed his stiff dick, ran her soapy fingers through his coarse pubic hair, and he groaned and leaned against the wall.

"How come people always want to have sex in the shower?"

she gasped as his fingers danced between her thighs. "It's hideously dangerous."

"You're kind of wrecking the mood, honey bear."

"I was just asking. Slippery surface, water everywhere, soap in sensitive places—it's a recipe for disaster."

"Honey, you think too much."

"Spoken like a true redneck asshole."

He laughed and pulled her close for a kiss. She nearly slipped out of his grip; they were like soapy seals. "I *am* a redneck asshole."

"As long as we've got that straight," she mumbled into his mouth as he cupped her face and kissed her with a thoroughness that made her forget about the general unsafe conditions.

He slid his hands over her butt, lifting her to him, and she could feel his strong hard-on pressing into her stomach. Water beat relentlessly down on them, making her think of a July rainstorm, all fury and heat.

He was kissing her neck, pressing her tightly against him, and she realized her feet were off the tiles. She wrapped her legs around his waist as he rubbed his dick through her lower lips, teasing her, caressing her, but she grabbed his hand and squeezed. He caught her subtle "fuck me now!" signal and carefully eased into her.

It was a tight fit—stupid water!—and she felt a little like a butterfly being pinned to a board. But it was glorious, all the same. She never wanted to be anywhere but where she was at that moment.

His head fell back so rapidly she heard the thunk! as it connected with the wall. He didn't appear to notice, just clutched at her and thrust, thrust, thrust. She hung on, kissing his shoulders, his neck, biting him, nibbling at the clean, slick skin.

"Oh boy," he groaned.

"Took the words right out of my mouth. Speaking of mouths. Put yours back on mine."

He obliged for a moment, then broke the kiss with a groan. "Honey, I'm gonna—owe—you—one."

"That's why God made beds." She laughed as he stiffened against her, as his head hit the wall again, as his eyes rolled back in his head. She feared he would drop her, then realized he'd never, ever drop her.

After a long moment he set her down on shaky legs, and bent to her, and kissed her softly, sweetly.

"You realize we've never done it in a bed?"

"Bet you won't be able to say that in the morning," he replied.

"How long do you think the hot water's going to hold out?" she asked.

"Long as we need it to. But let's get dry and I'll show you how fine I think you are."

"Sounds like a plan."

# Chapter 38

They didn't bother with towels, just rolled around on the bed and let the blankets dry them off. His mouth was everywhere: her mouth, her wet hair, her neck, her breasts. He suckled on her nipples until she thought she would lose her mind, kissed her stomach, licked her belly button.

Kissed her lower, harder, stuck out his tongue and tasted her for what felt like hours. Actually pushed his tongue inside her and wiggled it around until she was clutching his head and crying out at the ceiling.

He pulled back only slightly and licked, kissed, sucked. Stroked her with his tongue and his fingers, and when his tongue flicked across her throbbing clit while two fingers slipped inside her, she was afraid she'd hurt him, she was clutching at his head so hard. Her orgasm zoomed through her blood like a bullet, a sweet, dark bullet. Her heels drummed on the bed, and she was begging him to come up here and *fuck her now* and he just laughed against her slick flesh, laughed and stuck his tongue into her again, laughed and licked her and kissed her and held her apart for his mouth.

He enjoyed her the way a man in the desert would have

enjoyed a piece of fruit, savoring it and gobbling it at the same time.

At last, at last he stopped, came up to her, grabbed her by the shoulders and rolled her over. She straddled him at once, grabbed for him, guided him into her. So deep, he went into her so deeply and sweetly she could feel him in her heart— her heart, it was galloping, bursting, blowing up in her chest.

He grabbed her by the back of her neck and pulled her down, kissed her, forced her lips wide for his tongue, bit her, licked her, and she kissed him back and thrust against him, rode him, used him the way he was using her.

Now they were rolling over on the bed, now he was on top, now she was, and they were both talking at once and he was groaning and shouting and kissing her and touching her everywhere, and she held her to him as tightly as she could while the cords stood out on his neck and he roared at the ceiling and she didn't think until after what the guards outside must be thinking.

# Chapter 39

They talked. And talked and talked. About everything and nothing. The new Diet Coke, the old family. Charmer. C.O.P. O.S.I. The Boss. Tide versus Cheer. (For a soldier living life on the edge, he was surpassingly knowledgeable about laundry.) Fathers and daughters. Opening presents Christmas Day versus Christmas Eve.

In a halting voice almost unrecognizably thick, he told her one horrifying story after another. Horrifying and hilarious, sometimes. His family was as quick with the guns as they were to slip on banana peels. He told her about how he'd run from them for years, to the FBI, to the Snakepit.

She in turn talked about her father, still alive and well (she assumed; she hadn't seen him in three years, talked to him in nineteen months) in Cottage Grove.

"I bet he worries about you," he said.

"I bet you're wrong," she replied, and for a wonder, the old hurt had little power over her at the moment. Why that should be, she didn't know. Was it just Kevin? New opportunities? Mind-blowing sex? A lurid combination of the three?

"I bet he is, though."

"It's not like I'm going to find out," she replied, a little defensively.

He said nothing, just rubbed her knuckles across his lips.

"It's not the same thing," she continued as if he had argued with her. "You had a totally different thing with your fath—your family. My father and I—we were never close."

"Yup, but that's in your power to change. You could start to fix it with a phone call."

"Kevin, darling, you don't know what the hell you're talking about. I mean, you haven't seen your family in years, by choice, just like me. But you're telling me to plunk in a quarter and give Dear Old Dad a call? Do you hear yourself?"

"Yup, you're right, but you could still call him."

She resisted the urge to leap out of the bed and pace the small bedroom, so anonymous it might as well have been a Super 8 motel room. "If I called him, he would have zero interest in seeing me."

"Nope."

"What, nope? What does that even mean?"

"Don't get your Irish up," he replied mildly. "But you're wrong. Who could know you and never want to see you?"

She was warmly flattered, although he was wrong, wrong, wrong. "Kevin, it's possible that you don't see me—thank God—the way my father does."

"I hope not, honey. But you could still call him."

"I'm not calling him."

"Okay."

"Kevin, you just don't know. You had a relatively normal family life."

He laughed at her.

"Okay, your dad was—is—the head of the biggest crime syndicate south of the Mason-Dixon line, but he still came home every night for dinner, loved your mom, loved you and your brothers. Played catch with you, for God's sake. My dad—he isn't like that."

"People change."

"No," she replied. "They really don't."

"You'd better be wrong," he sighed, and kissed her hand again.

# Chapter 40

She woke up startled: where was she? What had happened?

She stretched, feeling pleasantly sore, pleasantly used. Tired, still, but in a really good way.

The incredible events of the past few days—hours!—came back to her, and she rested in the mussed bed, thinking about Kevin and smiling.

The smile faded as she sensed she was alone in the small house. Something about the air: you could always tell when nobody else was sharing space with you.

She turned her head, saw the note resting on the other pillow. Didn't move for a long minute, just stared at it.

*That's not going to be anything I want to read*, she thought.

She lay there for a long moment, cursing herself for her cowardice, and finally forced herself to reach out and pick it up. Her arm seemed to go on forever; her fingers finally, finally reached the piece of paper.

She thought: *He just ran out to get coffee. He'll be right back.*

She thought: *The Boss called and made him come in for a debriefing. He'll be right back.*

She thought: *He had a heart attack but didn't want to bother me, so he quietly called an ambulance for himself. He'll be back after ten days of observation.*

She picked it up and read it. Once was all she needed.

*Jenny, sweetie,*
 *I can't. Been alone too long. Besides, there's bad guys to catch. I'll never forget you.*

          *'Bye, honey,*
          *Kevin*

"Oh, you slick, sly son of a bitch," she said aloud, and threw the covers back.

# Chapter 41

*Eight days later*
*Prague*

"You'll meet your contact in five minutes. Show him the money; he'll give you the codes. You're not wired, so you'll have to remember it."

"I'll try," Kevin said dryly.

"Yeah, yeah, you're secretly a genius, which is why we're both freezing our asses off in a public park in the middle of the day."

"Temper," he said mildly.

"Anyway. Pop open your cell, give the codes to our tech guys. They'll fix it so the bad guys won't be able to arm the bomb."

"What about the others?"

"We've got a guy ready to track our little friend back to his bolt hole. So let him leave. Okay? Resist all urges to re-arrange his dental work. Are you reading me? You're reading me, right?"

Kevin almost smiled. If he *had* smiled, it would have been the first one in over a week.

"I know that look. Restrain the urge to pound on him until his face falls off. Hello? You listening?"

He couldn't get Jenny out of his mind. His thoughts varied from feeling like a total shitheap to feeling he had done the right thing: she would be safe now.

And if he was afraid, if he wasn't ready to have a family, to *endanger* a family, to suck her into the Stone family legacy of bumbling ruthlessness, so what? There were plenty of single fellas in the world. Nothin' meant nothin', as his daddy liked to say.

"I'll try," he said, "but it won't be easy. Little shit."

"Yeah, well, that's why we're going to stomp him good. He knows you from the Snakepit, and The Boss has kept a lid on it: most everybody thinks those pukes are still in business."

"You sure you don't want some action?"

"Are you kidding?" Caitlyn shook her head, pink strands of hair flying. "I'm only here for my second honeymoon. It is a *total* coincidence that there was, you know, a little errand to run also."

"For someone who doesn't work for The Boss, you and Dmitri sure do—"

"Oh, shut up," she said, and gave him a shove in the general direction of the park.


"Nobody wants gold anymore," he commented. "Too hard to move. And the price is too volatile."

"I'm an old-fashioned guy," the puke said. He was about five-eight, with chin-length blond hair and watery blue eyes. His hook-like nose dominated his face; his mouth was hidden by a straggly, dark-blond beard. He smelled like stale cheese. "You get how the code works? You can only punch it in once. And, obviously, if your finger slips, it's ka-boom Venice."

"It's sinking anyway," he said, and the puke laughed.

Kevin handed over the small, sleek briefcase. Caitlyn had picked it out in a small leather shop called, interestingly, Hobo Handbag. He had been indifferent. He was about most things, these days.

Had it only been a week since he'd snuck out on Jenny like a thief?

He didn't sneak, he reminded himself. He saved her.

From pure force of habit, he looked around the small park again. It was just a park: trees, bushes, cracked sidewalk. Almost empty—it was business hours, and school was in session. Nobody was close.

"Ready?" the puke asked.

"Yup."

"Six. Two. Twenty-two. Eighteen. Six. Six. Six."

"Got it."

"Here comes your tech."

"What?" Not part of the plan. Kevin heard the sharp clicking of heels on concrete and nearly fell over. It felt like every tendon in his neck was creaking. He had *just* looked, dammit—nobody could sneak up on him without serious outside support. *Set up!* his brain was screaming. He had about half a second to decide what to do, and if he guessed wrong, he'd—

"I'll take that code now," Jenny said, smiling at them both.

Kevin gaped. The puke was also gaping, more in admiration than the total shock that Kevin felt. Jenny was buried in a man's black wool coat which came past her knees. Her blond hair shone in the sun. One eyelid dropped in a wink.

"He's got it," the puke said helpfully.

Jenny's smile broadened. "Wonderful."

"You're pretty fine, lady. You up for some action later?"

"I'd rather," she said sweetly, "bathe in my own vomit."

"What?" the puke asked. Then, "Gaaaaaah!" as Dmitri came out of nowhere—literally. One minute it was the three of them, the next Dmitri was standing there, and put a hand on the back of his neck. To Kevin it looked like Dmitri was barely touching the guy, but everyone could hear the small bones in his neck creaking like a door on rusty hinges.

"A moment of your time?" Dmitri asked, smiling, and then hauled the puke deeper into the park.

"Uh," Kevin said, because honest to God, it was the only thing he could think of.

"Code," Jenny said, the smile plucked away as if it had been a mirage. She was holding a cell phone open, the small screen shining up into her face.

"Uh."

"Cooooooode," she repeated, with much less patience.

He took hold. Reminded himself he was a professional. Tried not to drool over the gorgeous little blonde in the big, black coat. Ohhhhhh, she looked good. She would always look good to him, even when she was eighty and wrinkled. Not that he was likely to see her eighty and wrinkled. He'd fixed that a week ago.

He reminded himself he was a professional. Dammit, hundreds of thousand of lives were in the balance!

*I wonder if she's wearing pink—*

"Six. Two. Twenty-two. Eighteen. Six. Six. Six."

"Got that?" she said to the phone, which beeped in reply. She slapped it shut.

"Uh," he said again. "So, how've you been?"

"Just fine."

Then she put a small foot directly into his groin, and the world disappeared in a black hole of pain, and the damp cement sidewalk rushed up at him as he collapsed.

"Idiot," she said as he gasped and rocked back and forth. "You do not leave me to 'save' me, got it? I'm not afraid to be a Stone, and I'm not afraid of your family. You think fabulous sex is simple to come by? You think two people bond like that so easily? That what we had happens every day?"

He made a small croaking noise.

"Right. I'm sticking around, chum, and so are you." She paused. "Sorry about your testicles."

He finally managed to get a breath. He lay on the wet concrete (at least, he thought with glum humor, it had stopped raining) and looked up at her. "I couldn't take it if something happened to you."

"That's because you're in love, asshole."

He smiled. "I am?"

"Yup." She stuck her hands in her coat pockets and glared down at him. "And for the record, the next time I wake up with a note, you'll be having it for lunch."

"I love you, too."

Her phone beeped and she looked at it. "Bad guy's in custody."

"Guess it all worked out, then."

"Guess so."

"Why'd you come after me?"

"Why d'you think?"

"It's a crummy life. I'm not fixing to retire anytime soon."

"Well," she said reasonably, "neither am I. I've been on the sidelines my whole life. Waiting to be the star in the movie, not the quiet, good-natured pal. Now I've got you. Romance, action, science fiction—it's all here, as long as I'm with you. Do you think I could give you up? Go back to answering phones and hearing about Caitlyn's adventures and wondering what it would be like to be the main event in my own life?"

"You're the main event in my life. You gonna help me up?"

She dug a small toe into his ribs. "Is that a euphemism for 'are we gonna go back to your hotel room now and do it for hours and hours'?"

"Yup," he said, and she stuck out a hand, which he grabbed like a lifeline, and she pulled him up, up, up into her arms.

# Part Three

# WITHAL*

*Defined by *Merriam-Webster* as: 1. together, with this.

# Epilogue

Caitlyn marched into The Boss's office, looking typically disheveled and pissed off. Hair the color of a daffodil. Ripped jeans. Dmitri was right behind her, inscrutable as ever. Brand-new (pressed!) jeans.

She stuck a finger in The Boss's face and said, "Don't have Jenny call my cell phone at four-thirty in the morning anymore."

"Don't answer it," The Boss replied, unmoved.

"And it's only because she asked that we're here."

"Right."

"Because, you've heard this before, right? We don't work for you. I. Run. A. Salon. He's. A. Count."

"I have a job, you know," Dmitri said mildly. "I don't spend the day being a count."

"Right, sweetie, your little computer thing." It rivaled Bill Gates's empire, but she never stopped calling it that. She ran her fingers through her hair, which had recently been cut brutally short and dyed bright yellow. "My point is, I don't want you reading anything into this."

"Never," The Boss said.

Dmitri pulled a chair out for his scowling bride, who flung herself into it with the grace of a dying moose.

The door opened again, and Kevin Stone, dressed in civvies, walked in.

"Say it ain't so! They got you, too?" Caitlyn gasped.

"Yeah, well." He shrugged. "Couldn't sleep, anyway. With Jenny's new schedule, seems like somebody's always awake."

"Do not get her started on Jenny's new schedule," Dmitri said hastily.

"Right. We doing this here, or in a conference room?"

"Here is fine. We're waiting on one more, and then we'll start the official debriefing."

"The bad guys aren't really going to blow up Hawaii, are they?"

"Not if we have anything to say about it."

"Didn't anybody notice they were fiddling around with all the volcanoes? I mean, that's bold. Hold an island hostage! A hundred billion or blammo."

"Hawaii is an archipelago," her husband pointed out gently.

"I knoooooooow," Caitlyn lied.

"So, lots of islands held hostage."

"Whatever it is, I'm in," Kevin said at once. He was leaning against The Boss's desk, ignoring the man's scowl. "I'll go right now."

"Thank you, Kevin, but we're looking for a team effort on this one."

"I've never been to Hawaii," Caitlyn admitted, which made her tall husband smile, a rare and wonderful thing. "Uh, totally off the subject, because I don't want you to misinterpret this as concern for you, because I have zero concern for you—it's only because you're married to my best friend that I even ask, but I'm still a little curious. How's your kid?"

"Incarcerated," he replied quietly.

Caitlyn had the grace to blush. "Oh. I—okay, that's a

tough one. Normally I'd say 'that's too bad', except she's hideously dangerous and should not be running around."

"Thank you," The Boss said, looking pleased.

"Stacy and I visited her last night for about an hour. Ironically, she had little interest in seeing us. If it wasn't for the glass separating us," he added thoughtfully, "she and my wife would have rumbled."

"Rumbled?" Dmitri and Kevin asked in unison.

"Well." Caitlyn nibbled her lower lip. "I guess—keep visiting? I mean, she let Kevin and Jenny get away. Came back with them to see you. That's good, right? She wanted to see you? Gave up the Snakepit to see you."

"Tried to kill my wife."

"To be fair, she was your fiancée at the time. Well, okay, that was bad. But look at all the good stuff that happened after!"

The Boss was rubbing his pale eyebrows and squinting over Caitlyn's shoulder. "Can someone please change the subject?"

He was ignored. "Besides, haven't you ever seen a toddler acting out? That's what Charmer's like: a mean, tall toddler. With split ends. Homicidal tendencies. And, um, really bad nails."

Dmitri leaned over and murmured in Caitlyn's ear and, quite out of character, she dropped the subject. "So what are we waiting for? Are we saving Hawaii or are we fingering ourselves?"

"You've really got a way with words," Kevin said. "You should write children's songs."

The door opened yet again, and in walked Jenny, laden with file folders, discs, and her laptop.

"Hi, babe," Kevin called cheerily.

"Nice of you to join us, Mrs. Stone."

Jenny didn't change expression, or cringe away; she had

The Boss's number, his weakness, and they all knew it. She went around the room, handing file folders to everyone, opening her laptop, getting settled in her chair.

Kevin leaned down and kissed her on the cheek, which caused roses to bloom in her cheeks, but she never looked up from her paperwork. He slouched into the seat beside her, booted heels resting comfortably on The Boss's recently polished desk.

"Make this quick," Caitlyn said. "I want to save Hawaii so I can get some beach time."

Kevin was playing with a lock of Jenny's hair; she absently swatted his hand away. Dmitri leaned forward and murmured in Caitlyn's ear again; she colored and giggled.

The Boss stared at them all, his expression unreadable, and then began the briefing.

*My new family,* The Boss reflected as he used a laser pointer on the wall map of Hawaii to highlight the threatened areas.

Not all of them would admit it, but this *was* a family now. Disappointed, betrayed by blood relatives, here was the real family. The family he had made. Ex-wife (dead), homicidal kid (locked up), new wife (asleep in bed). Co-workers . . . but somehow more.

Jenny Stone looked up and interrupted his presentation. *So much more polite than Caitlyn*, he mused, *but she still has no trouble expressing herself.* "Boss, one moment. I just got the latest intel off the S.A.T. line . . . we may need to adjust our plans . . ."

Caitlyn groaned. "This is going to take *longer*? Why did you just *say* all that stuff if it's not relevant?"

Jenny smiled at her old friend. "Not much longer. I promise."

"Can't you just say, 'Dmitri, Caitlyn, here's your flight info, here's where the bad guys are—fetch.' Can't you?"

"Next time," Jenny promised. She leaned over and snatched the laser pointer from The Boss. "My turn now."

"Okay," Jennifer said as she wrapped up their discussion about an hour later. "Mirage, Wolf, you'll be on point. Kevin and I will be coming in, too, posing as tourists."

"Oh, my poor Jenny," Caitlyn groaned, burying her face in her hands. "What he's brought you to! I could barf right now."

"Well, don't," O.S.I.'s newest member said. Her badge had her picture, along with the words *Jennifer B. Stone, Ops, Intel, Administration.* Her badge was green. At O.S.I., badges were white (entry level), pink (administrative assistants), lavender (scientists), navy blue (field ops), green (Ops, Intel, Admin), and black (The Boss).

Caitlyn and Dmitri insisted on retaining their freelance status, and eschewed badges altogether.

"And get going," she added as Caitlyn climbed to her feet, stretched, and groaned. "Think about all those poor innocent people in Hawaii."

"It's not that I don't care," Caitlyn protested, "it's that there's always poor innocent people being threatened by hideous marching death. And we always save them in the nick of time. At least this time we're going somewhere where the weather's nice."

"Going right now," Jenny added. "'Bye."

"Us, too?" Kevin asked.

"Yup. Don't worry, I packed plenty of sporks."

"Missed you last night," her husband said in a low voice, leaning over so far he nearly knocked her laptop to the floor.

Jenny smiled. "I booked us at the Hilton Hawaiian Village.

The honeymoon suite. We'll do what we always do—mix business with pleasure."

"Damn. A guy could fall in love."

"Not as fast as this girl," she said, gathering up her folders and closing the meeting.

Two lovers. And an unforgettable passion
that transcends time in
AGAIN
by Sharon Cullars.
Available now from Brava . . .

Inner resolve is a true possibility when temptation isn't within sight. Like the last piece of chocolate cheesecake with chocolate shavings; that last cigarette; that half-filled glass of Chianti . . . or the well-defined abs of a man who's had to take his shirt off because he spilled marinara sauce on it. Not deliberately. Accidents happen. At the sight of hard muscles, resolve flies right out of the window and throws a smirk over its wing.

Part of it was her fault. Tyne had offered him a shoulder rub, because during the meal he had seemed tense, and she'd suspected that his mind was still on the occurrences of the day. After dessert, he sat in one of the chairs in the living room while she stood over him. Even though he had put on a clean shirt, she could feel every tendon through the material, the image of his naked torso playing in her mind as her fingers kneaded the taut muscles.

As David started to relax, he leaned back to rest his head on her stomach. The lights were at half-dim. Neither of them was playing fair. Especially when a hand reached up to caress her cheek.

"Stop it," she whispered.

He seemed to realize he was breaking a promise, because the hand went down, and he said, "I'm sorry." But his head remained on her stomach, his eyes shut. From her vantage, she could see the shadow of hair on his chest. She remembered how soft it felt, feathery, like down. Instinctively, and against her conscious will, her hand moved to touch the bare flesh below his throat. She heard the intake of breath, felt the pulse at his throat speed up.

She told herself to stop, but there was the throbbing between her legs that was calling attention to itself. It made her realize she had lied. When she told him she wanted to take it slow, she had meant it. Then. But the declaration seemed a million moments ago, before her fingers touched him again, felt the heat of his flesh melding with her own.

He bent to kiss her wrist, and the touch of his lips was the catalyst she needed. The permission to betray herself again.

She pulled her hands away, and he looked up like a child whose treat had been cruelly snatched away. She smiled and circled him. Then slowly she lowered herself to her knees, reached over, unbelted and unbuttoned his pants. Slowly, pulled down the zipper.

"But I thought you wanted . . ." he started.

"That's what I thought I wanted." She released him from his constraints. "But right now, this is what I want." She took him into her mouth.

She heard an intake of breath, then a moan that seemed to reverberate through the rafters of the room. She felt the muscles of his thighs tighten beneath her hands, relax, tighten again. Her tongue circled the furrowed flesh, running rings around the natural grooves. She tasted him, realized that she liked him. Liked the tang of the moisture leaking from him. And the strangled animal groans her ministrations elicited.

There were pauses in her breathing, followed by strained exhalations. Then a sudden weight of a hand on the back of her head, guiding her. She took his cue, began sucking with a pressure that drew him farther inside her mouth. Yet there was more of him than she could hold.

He was moments from coming. She could feel the trembling in his limbs. But suddenly he pushed her away, disgorging his member from her mouth with the motion.

He shook his head. "No, not yet," he said breathlessly. "Why don't you join me?" Before she could answer, he stood up, pulling her up with him, and began unbuttoning her blouse, almost tearing the seed pearls in the process. The silk slid from her skin and fell to the ground in a languid pool of golden-brown. He hooked eager fingers beneath her bra straps, wrenched them down. Within seconds, she was naked from the waist up, and the current in the room, as well as the excitement of the moment teased her nipples into hard pebbles. His fingers gently grazed them, then he grazed each with his tongue. Her knees buckled.

"How far do you want to go?" he breathed. "Because I don't want you to do this just for me."

Her answer was to reach for the button of his shirt, then stare into those green, almost hazel eyes. "I'm not doing this for you. I'm being totally selfish. I want you . . . your body . . ." She pushed the shirt over his shoulders, yanked it down his arms.

"Hey, what about my mind?" he grinned.

She smiled. "Some other time."

They undressed each other quickly, and as they stood naked, his eyes roamed the landscape of her body with undeniable appreciation. Then without ceremony, he pulled her to the floor on top of him so abruptly that she let out an "oomph." His hands gripped the plump cheeks of her ass, began kneading the soft flesh. She felt his hardened penis against her stomach and began moving against it, causing him to inhale sharply. His hands soon stopped their kneading and replaced the touch with soft, whispery caresses that caused her crotch to contract with spasms. One of his fingers played along her crevice as his lips grabbed hers and began licking them. His finger moved to the delicate wall dividing both entryways, moved past the moist canal, up to her clitoris, started teasing her orb just as his tongue began playing along hers. She grounded her pelvis against him, desperately claiming her own pleasure, listening to the symphony of quickly pumping blood, and intertwined breaths playing in her ears.

He guided her onto his shaft. Holding her hips, he moved her up, down, in an achingly slow and steady pace that was thrilling and killing, for right now she thought she could die with the pleasure of it, the way he filled her, sated her. She felt her eyes go back into her head (she had heard about the phenomenon from other bragging women, and had thought they were doing just that—bragging. But now she knew how it could happen.)

"Ooooh, fuck," she moaned.

"My thoughts exactly," he whispered back, and with a deft motion, changed their positions until he was on top of her. Straddled on his elbows, he quickened his thrusting, causing a friction that drove her to a climax she couldn't stop. Her inner walls throbbed against the invading hardness, and she drew in shallow breaths as her lungs seemed to shatter with the rest of her body.

She put her arms around his waist and wrapped her legs around his firm thighs. His body had the first sheen of perspiration. She stroked along the dampness of his skin, then reciprocated the ass attention with gentle strokes along his cheeks.

"I want . . . I want . . . " he exerted but couldn't seem to finish the sentence. Instead, he placed his mouth over hers until she was able to pull his ragged breaths into her needy lungs. The wave that washed over her once had hardly ebbed away before it began building again. Now his pace was frantic, his hips pounding her body into the carpeting, almost through the floor. Not one for passivity, she pounded back just as hard and eagerly met each thrust. The wave was gathering force, this one threatening a cyclonic power that would rip her apart, render her in pieces. She didn't care. His desperation was borne of sex, but also she knew, of anger and frustration. He was expelling his demons inside her, and she was his willing exorcist . . .

*Blood was everywhere. On the walls, which were already stained with vile human secretions; on the wooden floor, where the viscous fluid slowly seeped into the fibers of the wood and pooled between the crevices of the boards. Soon, the hue would be an indelible telltale witness of what had happened, long after every other evidence had been disposed of. Long after her voice stopped haunting his dreams. Long after he was laid cold in his grave.*

*He bent to run a finger through one of the corkscrew curls. Its end was soaked with blood. The knife felt warm in his hands still. Actually, it was the warmth of her life staining it.*

*He turned her over and peered into dulled brown eyes that accused him in their lifelessness. Gone was the sparkle—sometimes mischievous, sometimes amorous, sometimes fearful—that used to meet him. Now, the deadness of her eyes convicted him where he stood, even if a jury would never do so. The guilt of this night, this black, merciless night, would hound his waking hours, haunt his dreams, submerge his peace, indict his soul. There would now always be blood on his hands. For that reason alone, he would never allow himself another moment of happiness. Not that he would ever find it again. What joy he would have had, might have had, lay now at his feet in her perfect form. Strangely, in death, she had managed to escape its pall. Her skin was still luminescent, still smooth. If it weren't for the vacuous eyes, the blood soaking her throat, the collar of her green dress, the dark auburn of her hair . . . he might hold to the illusion that somewhere inside, she still lived.*

*He reached a shaky hand to touch her cheek. It was warm, soft, defying death even as it stiffened her body.*

*He bent farther, let his lips graze hers one last time. Their warmth was a mockery. Her lips were never this still beneath his. They always answered his touch, willingly or not.*

*He saw a tear fall on her face, and for a second was confused. It rolled down her cheek and mixed with the puddle of blood. He realized then that he was crying. It scared him. He hadn't cried since he was a child. But now, another tear fell, and another.*

*Through his grief, he knew what he would have to do. She was gone. There was no way to bring her back. Her brother would be searching for her soon. She wasn't an ordinary Negress. She was the daughter of a prominent Negro publisher, now deceased, and the widow of a prominent Negro lawyer. She had a place in their society. So, yes, she would be missed. There would be a hue and cry for vengeance if it were ever discovered that she had been murdered.*

*Which was why he could not let her be found.*

*He knew what he had to do. It wasn't her anymore. It was just a body now. Yet, he couldn't resist calling her name one last time.*

*"Rachel."*

*Then he began to cry in earnest.*

Tyne pushed through the sleep-cloud that fogged her mind. The dream-world still tugged at her, reached out cold fingers to pull her back. But her feet ran as fast as they could, ran toward the name hailing her, pleading with her to hurry. The name reverberated around . . . *Rachel . . . Rachel . . . Rachel . . .*

"Rachel . . . Rachel . . . "

The sound woke her. She slowly opened her eyes, lay there for a moment, not remembering. Gradually, disorientation gave way to familiarity. Shaking off sleep, she became aware of her surroundings. Recognized the curtains that hung at the moon-bathed window, saw the wingback chair that was a silhouette in front of it. Sometime during the night or early morning, he had retrieved her clothes and laid them neatly on the chair's back.

He was shifting in his sleep, murmuring. Then she heard the name again, just as she had heard it in her dream. "Rachel." He strangled on the syllables, his voice choked with emotion—with . . . grief, she realized. She sat up, turned. His back was to her, shuddering. He was crying . . . in his sleep. Was calling to a woman—a woman named Rachel. Someone he'd never mentioned before. And obviously a woman who meant a lot to him, and whose loss he freely felt in his unconscious state. So he'd lied about never having been in love. But why?

A pang of jealousy moved through her, pushed away affection, gratification. She didn't want to be solace for some lost love he was still pining for. Didn't want to be a second-hand replacement to someone else's warmth in his bed. She looked over at the clock. It was almost four anyway. She might as well get home to get ready for work.

She shifted off the mattress delicately, grabbed her clothes from the chair and started for the door. She would dress downstairs to make sure she didn't wake him. She turned at the door to look at him. The shuddering had stopped. There was only the peaceful up and down motion of deep breathing. She opened the door, shut it lightly and made her escape.

Here's a look at
AND ABLE
by Lucy Monroe.
Available now from Brava . . .

Hotwire's blue eyes burned with sexy challenge. "I want a kiss, Claire . . . Are you going to give it to me?"

"Sure." She went up on her toes, intent on bussing his cheek.

He turned his head just enough, though, and her lips ended up pressed lightly to his. She didn't open her mouth, but she didn't pull away immediately as she'd planned to, either. She hung there, suspended by the connection between their mouths, her body humming with excitement. One second the kiss was soft and light, and the next he yanked her against his hard, male body and his mouth slammed down over hers with definite intent.

He took her mouth with the skill and power of an invading army . . . or one very formidable mercenary.

The man certainly knew how to kiss. He ate at her lips until she was dizzy from the pleasure of it. His fingers massaged her jaw, as if encouraging her complete surrender, the only kind she was sure he recognized. She'd never experienced anything so amazing in her life as Hotwire's kiss. She moaned out her approval while gripping the front of his white silk dress shirt in her fists.

He growled something she could not understand against

her lips and then his hands skimmed down, over her naked shoulders and around to the exposed skin of her back. His fingertips touched bare skin between the velvet lacing and played tantalizingly with the bow.

Man alive, what would she do if he untied it? She'd read about being branded by a man's touch, but had never known what it meant . . . until now. Her skin grew hot under his fingers, so hot she would swear burn marks would be left behind. Only it didn't hurt like a burn.

It felt too darn good for her sanity.

Without really thinking about it, she opened her mouth. His tongue tangled instantly with hers and took immediate and absolute possession of the interior of her mouth. Pleasure jolted through her body, spearing her right between her legs and she arched her pelvis toward him.

His hands traveled down over her bottom to the backs of her legs below her skirt hem, then came up under her skirt and back up her legs. She almost jumped out of her skin when he touched the sensitive flesh of her inner thighs. He curled his big fingers around them, holding her while his thumbs kneaded her bottom and he lifted her into closer contact with his body.

She undulated against him in a move that felt entirely natural, but froze in shock as her mound brushed against the hard roll of his erection.

He wasn't so inhibited. He used his grip on her to move her up and down the length of his engorged and rigid penis, making a low, masculine sound of pleasure as he did so. Tremors more powerful than a Richter 10 earthquake went off inside her.

"Stop trying to seduce my maid of honor, Hotwire. It's time to throw the bouquet." Josette's voice crashed through the passionate haze surrounding Claire, bringing her back to reality with a thud.

What in the world had she been doing?

Hotwire jolted like a man shocked by a live electric wire and broke the kiss, practically tossing Claire away from him. She tottered on her unfamiliar heels and almost fell. He reached out to steady her, his expression pained, but snatched his hands back the moment she stopped wobbling.

The silence between them was more charged than the air after an electric storm.

"You have five minutes and then I'm tossing the bouquet," Josette said, her gaze faintly amused and assessing, before she turned to head back to the reception.

It would take Claire five minutes just to get her breath back. How was she supposed to walk back into the reception following that?

After several more seconds of charged silence, he said, "I'm sorry. That was way out of line."

"I liked it."

Take a peek at Lori Foster's "Luscious" in
BAD BOYS OF SUMMER.
Coming in June 2006 from Brava!

The knock on the door startled Bethany Churchill so that she almost fell off the couch. With blurry eyes, she squinted at the kitchen clock on the far wall. Barely seven A.M.! Another glance at her sister's bedroom door showed that Marci slept on.

Wrapping herself in the borrowed sheet, Bethany hauled herself off the couch and went to the door. She put one eye to the peephole, and moaned at the sight before her.

Big, tall, sexy male.

No, no, no. She didn't need this, not today, not right now, not before caffeine.

Without opening the door, she called out, "What do you want, Luscious?" Her teeth snapped down on her tongue and she mentally cursed. "I mean, *Lucius*."

At the sound of his deep laugh, her head hit the door with a thump. Damn the other women in the building for giving him that ridiculous nickname. So he was SWAT. And brave. And he looked downright luscious. Luscious Rider, they called him, a name that seemed strangely apropos to her sleepy brain.

Not that Lucius, the egomaniac, ever complained over

the endearment. Nope, he soaked in female adoration as if
it were his due.

"Bethany, I take it?"

How could he always tell them apart? More than one guy
had been confused over time. More than one guy had insisted he didn't have a preference, as if she and her twin
were interchangeable, especially if Marci proved unavail-
able.

But not Lucius.

He behaved very differently with each of them.

Issuing an obvious challenge, Bethany said, "Yeah, so?"

"Open the damn door."

"Why?"

*His* head hit the wood this time. "I need to see Marci.
Now open up."

Of course he wanted to see Marci. The men always
wanted to see Marci. Her twin had a charisma that somehow hadn't entered Bethany's gene pool. "No, she's asleep."
*And I'm in my underwear, and I haven't yet recouped enough from
a bad week and a long night to face you.*

Another couple of hours sleep, at least three cups of coffee, *then* she might be ready to square off with the hunky
landlord.

A hesitation, then, "When did you get in, Bethany?"

Uh-oh. She knew that tone of his, a tone he never used
with Marci. "Midnight. Why?"

"You realize you're breaking the rent agreement by im-
posing on your sister so often."

*Screw yourself, Sergeant,* she mimed to herself—but she
didn't dare say the words aloud. After all, he was the landlord, and Marci really liked her apartment. "I'm only here
for a few days." Or weeks. Maybe even forever, if she didn't
find her backbone. "No big deal."

"It will be a big deal if you don't open the door."

"It's early."

*"And I have an emergency."*

Now more awake, Bethany put her eye to the peephole again. Lucius looked rumpled and tired, but in a good, cozy and warm way—not panicked. Definitely not injured. Her suspicions rose. "What kind of emergency?"

From behind Bethany, Marci yawned, then said, "What's going on?"

Well shoot. They'd awakened her sister. "I don't know." She glanced over her shoulder at Marci. "It's Lucius. He wants in for some reason."

"I have an emergency," Lucius yelled, proving the paper-thin walls did little to protect privacy.

Also in a T-shirt and underwear, Marci strode forward and edged Bethany aside. As if Lucius Ryder saw her in a state of undress every day, Marci opened the locks, removed the chain, and swung the door wide without a hint of modesty.

It was then that Bethany detected the beastly howling coming from Lucius's apartment across the hall.